Infusions

Java Writers

Java Writers

Copyright 2012 © Java Writers

All stories are works of fiction and any resemblance to real life characters, whether living or dead, is coincidental.

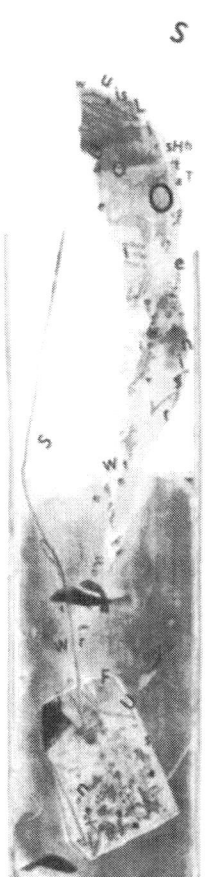

INFUSIONS
AN ANTHOLOGY BY JAVA WRITERS

Java Writers

Infusions

Introduction

The following poems and stories were written during a summertime writing workshop. Each piece has been through two rigorous sessions of group critique, with feedback from the rest of us on everything from verb tense to musicality of language to the story's point of view. It has been wonderful to watch each piece blossom into the fully realised work you will find in these pages. In many cases, the group's input concerned wanting *more*. More suspense! More playfulness! More poetry! More wickedness!

My favourite times in these workshops (indeed, in any workshop) were when a writer questioned lines of her own work, only to be told that the part she'd queried was the favourite part of everyone else. The lines that set the pulse for the rest of the piece. This occurs when writers stop looking over their shoulders and write exactly what they hear in their heads – silences included. This is what we really mean when we speak reverently about a writer's *voice*. We mean when they start to be themselves on the page. It's a thrilling moment for reader and writer alike.

The writers in this group met in writing classes I've taught over the last few years. They don't have a great deal in common with each other. They gravitated toward each other, I think, because they each take their writing extremely seriously while not taking themselves seriously at all. This is the best possible combination of traits for a writer. It means you can get a lot of work done and have a lot of laughs, while getting stuck in few ego driven dramas, which will only waste time and energy you could use for the work.

As well as continuing in classes, the group began to meet weekly (in Java café here in Galway) to share work and cheer each other on. In the time they have worked together each has done his own thing and achieved many goals. Some have had individual pieces published and done well in competitions. Some have given public readings of their work. A couple have self-published novels, to acclaim. Quite a few are working on larger projects as we speak.

From their time together, they receive support, critical feedback and the urging to go on, to embrace new challenges. They are strong creative individuals who stand stronger still as a group. You will see this as you read these selections – the way the poetry of one piece bumps along happily with the colloquialisms of another, the way that Irish characters mingle with those of other nations, the way small, tender moments and shocking plot twists walk hand in hand, companionably, through these pages.

Enjoy being in the company of these engaged and engaging writers. I do –at every session.

Susan Millar DuMars

Infusions

Java Writers

Infusions

Contents:

1. Redeeming Jesus by Fiona Scoble
2. The Shift by A. P. Kenny
3. The River by J.G. Lacey
4. Galway Hookers and other poems by Flish McCarthy
5. Dear Diary: 1965 by Duana Sala
6. Karma by Margaret Brady
7. A Funny Thing by Bern Butler
8. Te Quiero by Phillipa Maguire
9. Don't mention it by Bernadette Whyte
10. An Indian Summer by Lorna Moynihan
11. Swimming with the sprat and other poems by Ann Flynn
12. Dance into Danger by Yvonne McEvaddy
13. God's Gift by Evelyn Parsons
14. Haiku by Fleur Finlay

Java Writers

Infusions

Illustrations

Title page illustrations

Redeeming Jesus by Fiona Scoble
The Shift by Fiona Scoble
The River by Lara Luxardi
Galway Hookers by Fiona Scoble
Dear Diary: 1965 by Lara Luxardi
Karma by Lara Luxardi
A Funny Thing by Bern Butler
Te Quiero by Phillipa Maguire
Don't mention it by Fiona Scoble
An Indian Summer by Lara Luxardi
Swimming with the sprat by Lara Luxardi
Dance into Danger by Fiona Scoble
God's Gift by Evelyn Parsons

Cover design by Lara Luxardi

Type-setter Matt McEvaddy

Java Writers

Infusions

Redeeming Jesus
Fiona Scoble

Lawrence Wilkins was not a good man. In fact he was terrific at being not a good man. He was one of those few people who master self-ignorance to such a degree that he considered himself the salt of the earth, writing off every terrible thing he did as just sensible business, or good-natured trickery, or the act of a stunningly able underdog who everyone secretly roots for.

People never saw Lawrence's not-goodness coming because he owned a beautiful art gallery. He dazzled his victims with works of art before taking his bite. If the art wasn't enough then he used his eyes, which were remarkably round and blue. Whenever he was in a confrontation he'd make them as wide and round as possible and ogle down his opponent until they got dizzy. He also used them to control the young women he hired for the shop, goggling his wide eyes up and down and around them until they felt naked and never answered back.

Thanks mostly to previous owners, Lawrence's gallery had a marvellous reputation. His customers would journey for hours to revisit the dainty porcelain, cosy pottery, intricate jewels and myriad paintings from artists they'd been fond of for decades. Lawrence would flutter around them pointing out the most expensive pieces. If he particularly wanted to flatter a customer he'd whip out a bottle of flattish Champagne and offer a glass, then while they browsed he'd hammer the cork back in again, maintaining it for the next attempt. Often if a visitor had particularly liked a piece but hadn't bought it, Lawrence would nip back after they'd left and pencil in an extra £50 or so on the item, ready for next time.

One of the customers who'd long loved the gallery was the local priest, Father Murray. He had a soft spot for teapots, especially those satisfyingly weighty ones with thick glazes. He'd visited the gallery many times over the years and collected a substantial array, and he continued to visit despite the change of ownership and the uncomfortable habit the current owner had of staring so intensely. So when the church finally granted him the two thousand pounds he'd begged for to replace his altar's crumbling crucifix, he clipped up his black trousers and cycled right over to commission the work.

On seeing the priestly ankles draw up at his shop, Lawrence began to reach down for the Champagne, but then he remembered that last time he'd come the priest had only bought a cheap teapot so he stood up again.

"Ah! Lovely to see you again Father. Back for another... teapot?" Lawrence smiled guardedly.

"No, not today thanks. But I've got some brilliant news. I've finally got some funding for a new crucifix for the church, and I'd love if you could hand the job onto one of your artists."

Lawrence drew back his lips in a smile. "Well, what a piece of news! I've got a simply divine carpenter - excuse the pun! - on the books. He doesn't come cheap, but I'm sure he could put together a beautiful thing for you for, oh, say, oh how much do you have?"

"Two thousand," said the priest.

"Yes, yes about two thousand. I mean, he might usually ask for more, but I'm sure for a man such as yourself..." Lawrence nodded and swung back and forward on his heels. "Champagne?"

The minute the priest left, Lawrence phoned his man: a soft, quiet, self-taught carpenter who lived with his wife and eight daughters and hid all day in the shed with his tools.

Lawrence considered himself a patron of the arts, which in his case meant patronising artists as if they didn't know a damn thing until they wobbled and gave him their work at half the original price.

"James!" Lawrence barked ebulliently when the man's gentle voice answered. "Got a bit of work for you. Not a lot of money in it, but good for your soul young man. Can you handle a half-metre cross? Give it some fancy detail and whatnot? Can't give you more than a hundred but I'm sure you'll earn more for it in Heaven." He paused to blink while James muttered his answer. "Excellent! Hurry along with it won't you."

Slamming down the phone, Lawrence threw on his hat and strode out to the train station. He caught the first train to Harringham, a town about fifty kilometres away, which was famous for cream teas and dog races, but most importantly for its huge bric-a-brac, antiques and curios market.

Markets like this one could take days to navigate, but when a man like Lawrence has a mission, crowds part. He peered and pushed and prodded, ogling over people's heads and goggling round their shoulders until he spotted exactly what he was looking for.

The small, exhausted figure hung his head in repose as his neck sunk between strained shoulders. Lawrence picked him up round the legs and turned him over. His varnished wooden skin was warm from being under the sun all day. He was in good nick. None of his thorns were chipped, and even on the fiddly bits where the nails went in no toes or fingers were missing. There was just one flaw; as Lawrence pressed his thumb into the crook of the man's right knee he felt a sudden roughness, possibly a clump of varnish or a slip of the knife. He tilted him upside down to look at his face. The heavy eyelids and mouth were closed in silent prayer, faultless.

"How much?" Lawrence leaned his height over the small old woman behind the stall and opened his eyes wide at her. She was the typical sort of body you find behind bric-a-brac stalls, but not the canny sort of mind. She shrugged her rounded shoulders under her bright mismatching woollens.

"Oh," she began.

"I mean it can't be much," Lawrence enthused. "A crucifixion without a crucifix, and see here, a terrible knock behind this knee. I'll only take him for the sentiment." His large eyes riveted her tighter.

"Eighty pounds?" the lady enquired from behind thick glasses.

"Thirty."

"Seventy?"

"Thirty-five!" Lawrence drew up his full height and swept his now almost perfectly circular eyes over hers.

"Sure!" She flinched, and wrapped Jesus up in some tissue paper for safekeeping. Lawrence travelled home congratulating himself on getting one over the shrewd gypsy in the woollens.

Back at his gallery Lawrence carefully wrote out his finances.

£2,000
Minus £100 for the cross
Minus £35 for Jesus
(Minus £20 for the train)
Leaves a sweet £1,845 profit.

Infusions

He underscored the final figure then spun in his swivel chair and glared triumphantly at the painting behind the desk, which couldn't cower because it was already flat against the wall.

It was a week later, and a couple of days after Lawrence had received James's beautifully wrought cross, magnanimously passed him one hundred pounds, glued his bric-a-brac Jesus onto it, and handed it to Father Murray in exchange for the crisp two thousand, that Lawrence was watching Art Hunt and turned extremely pale.
"… and the figure was last tracked here, to Clare Booker's stall at this large bustling market." The presenter cast a tall and natty shadow over dumpy Clare Booker, enveloped in different outrageously coloured woollens but instantly recognisable.
"I had no idea!" Clare shrugged. "I can only tell you I sold it on about a week ago to some podgy bloke, and he didn't half drive a hard bargain, but I can't remember more!"
A photograph of Lawrence's Jesus took over the screen.
"The previous owner," the presenter explained, "an antiques dealer, failed to recognise the work, which can be identified by a distinctive signature etched into the wood of the crucified Jesus' right knee. Art historians are certain that this is in fact the signature of a more recent artist attempting to take credit for Michelangelo's original work. The piece is currently valued at two and a half million pounds."
It was a long, chill silence before Lawrence was able to exhale. He felt like his bones had gone cold. He got to his feet and reached his drinks cabinet where he poured a large whisky and leant over the wood willing his brain to act. *It's so miserably unfair!* His brain cried, voicing its instinctive self-pity. Then, *I'll meet the priest. I'll tell him there's an error with the work and I need to replace the figure. I'll get*

him a beautiful (inexpensive) replacement while I take what is rightfully mine to the auction house. All will be well! Lawrence repeated this mantra throughout the remainder of the evening while he sank his whisky, occasionally wallowing in the injustice of the world, occasionally sketching diagrams of the mansion he would build in the Seychelles if things worked out as they should.

Lawrence woke with first light, having slept fitfully. A mixture of whisky and personal vitriol at his predicament made his mouth taste like he'd been sucking old coins. He left his bed and brewed tea downstairs, then sipped it and eyeballed the birds in his garden until they hid in longer grass, forcing himself to wait until midmorning and to casually saunter into the church.

Finally, just before 11am, Lawrence left the hazy morning and stepped through the cool pews. He craned around to spot Father Murray, but the church seemed to be empty. As he realised this Lawrence quickened his steps towards the pulpit and searched for the crucifix, entertaining the first wisps of thought that perhaps he might not need to meet with the priest at all in order to solve this. *An open church, any vagrant could walk in, an anonymous owner for the auction...* his mind snaked ahead.

    Here it was! Lawrence saw the top of the cross resting high on the pulpit. He turned and paced briskly up the steps to where the priest would usually address the congregation, and found – *No!* – an empty cross resting in front of him. In shock he picked up the heavy cross and turned it around, furiously willing Jesus to be hanging on the other side. It was bare, and as his eyes rounded, aghast, he heard a clatter of crockery in the sacristy. Father Murray walked in before Lawrence could put down the cross.

Father Murray stopped still as he and Lawrence's wide eyes met. The priest's face went momentarily slack with glassy observation.

"Lawrence, lovely to see you here," Father Murray suddenly gathered his cheeks up into a smile and walked towards him. "I can't thank you enough for your artist's beautiful work. Do you know, the Bishop came by the day you delivered it, and was so admiring that he's borrowed it for display."

Lawrence looked down at the cross he clasped in his hands. "As you can see, we've got a short term replacement, just no figure for now," the priest continued.

He couldn't be certain as he hadn't looked closely at James' work, but Lawrence felt that he held the very same cross. He glanced at the priest.

"Well you see, in fact the artist wasn't so happy with the figure, and he's asked me to return it to him so he can fix you up with a new one. No extra charge of course!" Lawrence beamed.

"Oh don't be silly," smiled Father Murray. "It's a stunning job, and sure if I can't notice a thing wrong with it then the congregation won't. They'll all be thrilled to worship alongside it once the Bishop returns it in a couple of weeks."

"Really, I couldn't," Lawrence began, but the priest interrupted. "Now, that man's work was worth every bit of the two thousand you charged and I won't have him spend any more time on it."

Lawrence began to feel his heart pulsing on his ribs. He sized the priest up with a stately ogle, made more powerful by his position at the pulpit, and masked his suspicion with a warm "Ha!" He put down the cross and descended to the priest.

"Well Father, that's most kind of you. In that case let's discuss another idea I've had about putting on a charity exhibition in the church. Let's talk now over tea. You don't seem too busy."

The priest smiled shallowly. "That's so kind of you, Lawrence. I suppose we can't let such a kind gesture lie." He placed his arm around Lawrence's back and guided him towards the adjoining door.

Lawrence had a moment alone in the sacristy while the priest searched for the key to the church meeting room. He hesitated briefly before having a quick rifle through the white and purple robes hanging beside the door, checking whether his Jesus had been somehow stowed in their folds. There was little else to search through. A few of the priest's frivolous teapot collection adorned the windowsill and the shelf by the sink. One cupboard stood unopened; Lawrence tested the door and, feeling it give, opened it wide and stuck his head in to look. It was stuffy with incense and light glinted off the ornate brass thurible and from the red depths of sacramental wine bottles, but there was nothing else to see except the large Tupperware box of communion wafers waiting for a blessing. Lawrence was about to squat down and peer through the clear plastic, just to be sure, when he heard the jangle of keys and, too canny to be caught twice, quickly closed the cupboard door and stood by the window.

"Tea then?" asked the priest, and led Lawrence to the meeting room. He filled two mugs from a sturdy Burco boiler in the corner and fished out the teabags. *Too cheap even to brew in one of his precious teapots* Lawrence sneered to himself as he scanned the room, seeing no clue to his treasure's whereabouts. He began to concoct the exhibition he now had to explain, but was soon interrupted by a slight figure tapping at the doorframe and sitting down beside him.

"This is Mrs Jakes," the priest introduced her. "My greatest helper."

Infusions

Lawrence rolled his eyes over Mrs Jakes, taking in her thin hair, pudding face, and dull blouse, and decided she didn't warrant further looking.

"I'm collecting for the church raffle!" She rushed the words at Lawrence. "I've just bought a couple of tickets for myself. Would you like to take one? All for a good cause! Just five pounds!"

The priest smiled over his mug. "Great idea! Here's the perfect start to your charitable idea, Lawrence," he enthused.

Lawrence blanched. He skirted his eyes desperately one more time around the room, to no avail. "Oh, yes. Of course. Glad to help." Against every instinct, he forced his hand to reach into his wallet, unclasp a fiver, and bring the note gingerly to Mrs Jakes' waiting fingers. He watched the further five pound loss pocketed as he had his name noted and was handed the worthless ticket. Some mean wire inside him came suddenly to breaking point. He swept up from the chair so briskly that Mrs Jakes jumped off her seat.

"Well, it's been lovely, Father! I'll have to meet with you another time about the exhibition I'm afraid. Time presses!" He glowered and strode back into the morning, boiling with fury.

The priest waited until Mrs Jakes had left before he returned to the sacristy, walked to the windowsill, and lifted a quilted tea cosy to reveal Jesus stood in the huge green teapot normally reserved for meetings. The poor figure looked quite ungainly as his arms, jutting awkwardly at right angles to his body, protruded above the teapot's rim, and his melancholy face appeared to contemplate the tannin-stained innards below. It was not an ideal resting place, but the priest had only had seconds to hide him, having just scraped the glue from the cross when he spotted Lawrence heading through the churchyard.

"Sorry Lord," Father Murray muttered, as he lifted Jesus out of the pot and held him gently under the light to take a better look at the work. The perfect form and delicate features were indeed stunning, and yes there, behind the knee, was the telltale signature nicked into the wood.

It was fortunate that he'd had a free evening to catch Art Hunt or he might never have realised what had come into his possession. He hadn't needed to overcome much reasonable doubt to believe what Lawrence had done. He had worried about him since noticing that one of his favourite teapots in the shop seemed to double in price every couple of weeks.

He smiled as he imagined the moment when he could redeem the Jesus figure to its rightful place among other revered works of art at a gallery or museum. He already planned to put aside at least two thousand of whatever money the church gained from it to personally locate and commission Lawrence's carpenter to make a replacement.

Father Murray didn't see Lawrence again until the following weekend, by which time he had passed the Jesus figure on to experts and the church had taken over handling the situation. Lawrence appeared on the fifth page of the local paper, his bulbous face printed beside an article describing how he was charged with harassing and trespassing on the property of a local Bishop.

The priest snorted as he imagined the scene of Lawrence accusing the bemused Bishop of harbouring Jesus. *I'll be sure to take a holiday when the church goes to press about the Michelangelo discovery,* he thought.

Once he'd finished the paper, Father Murray walked round to the small green where the church's summer fundraising fair was starting. Mrs Jakes met him by the cupcake stand and led him to a central table on which rested their battered wooden tombola.

Infusions

"Welcome to our summer fair!" the priest called in his sunny voice, honed for such occasions. "We'll start by announcing the grand prize winner from our raffle!"

Though the parish wasn't huge, they'd managed to raise a tidy sum for the prize. The priest spun the handle and opened the hatch to draw out a ticket. LAWRENCE WILKINS it said.

The priest looked at the ticket. His teeth clamped tight in front of his tongue. *Judge not...* his mind announced one of its usual adages. He pressed his thumb hard on the paper and rubbed it, watching the ink begin to smudge. *Ugh that man's bad through and through; it's written through his body like in a stick of Blackpool rock.* He looked up at the small crowd gathered to watch the announcement, and his eyes caught those of his helper. "Would you believe it Mrs Jakes?" he grinned. "You won!"

Java Writers

The Shift
A. P. Kenny

According to the Oxford dictionary the word shift is a verb that means:
to put something aside and replace it by another or others; change or exchange: to shift friends; to shift ideas.
or
to transfer from one place, position, person, etc., to another: to shift the blame onto someone else.
or
to change gears in a manual transmission car.

In Ireland it also means making out, French kissing, snogging – call it what you like. If an Irish person says they "shifted" someone, it doesn't mean they shoved them off a bench or moved them from one place to another, it means they had some sort of a romantic encounter.

In the old days these romantic encounters usually happened in the local ballroom. Dances were usually held on Sunday nights, plus an odd weeknight, and were run by various organisations such as the Gardaí, nurses, or teachers.

In those days, men and women lined opposite sides of the hall. They eyed each other up and down, the males trying to catch the attention of the ladies they fancied, while the ladies did vice versa. The band announced "Next dance" after every three tunes. If a girl was not asked she had to sit it out like a wallflower, smoking a cigarette and pretending like she hadn't a care in the world. In contrast most of the men who were refused just kept on asking different girls until they finally got a yes.

The girls usually knew who they wanted to invite them to dance and more importantly who they did not want an invite from. They used different methods of refusing to accompany a man onto the floor. Many made a mad dash to the cloakroom if the wrong fellow was getting too close.

Some just said "No, Thank you," and looked away.

Often approached by a male with the question "Are you dancing?" others replied, "No, it's just the way I stand". Some of the girls who had come home from Dublin for the weekend thought they were smart when they said:

"I'm sweatin' Misther, ask me pal."

The more sophisticated girls always knew how to get the guy of their choice. They dressed well, had great poise, winked at the object of their desire and licked their lips at the same time. They always got their man.

Other hurdles had to be overcome when you got on the dance floor. The first was conversation.

"Do you come here often?" was a definite no-no opener. "Only when there's a dance on," was the usual response to this.

Then there was the dancing ability. The better dancers usually moved to an area called "Scrubber's corner". This was not an area associated with domestic helpers, but where the jiving and jitterbugging took place. Occasionally the manager of the ballroom came along, tapped dancers on the shoulder and pointed to the sign:

NO JIVING OR JITTERBUGGING ALLOWED.

His orders were obeyed for a few minutes but were ignored once his back was turned.

The local Parish priest turned up at the parochial dances. He ignored the jiving and jitterbugging but was very visible during the slow dances, walking around the floor making sure that there was the width of a sod of turf between the male and female bodies during the dance.

The third hurdle was the man's prospects. "He has a car." That was the most important condition. If he had a car he probably had a good job and at least the girl and her friends were ensured a lift home.

The shift usually took place during the dance and if some or all of the above conditions were in place. The man invited the girl for a mineral, a soft drink, usually lemonade or orange. There was no alcohol in those days. The sixties did not arrive in Ireland until the seventies. If the invitation was accepted they continued to dance together for the remainder of the evening. The gentleman then asked the girl to accompany him outside. I am talking about rural Ireland here where cars were in short supply. This was when the snogging etcetera took place. The action usually stopped short of doing anything that would have to be told in confession the following Saturday.

There were different types of shifters, both male and female. The serial shifters shifted someone different every time and liked bragging to their friends of their conquests. There was the older type, who was usually looking for a partner for life and felt time was running out so settled for less than their ideal and hoped for the best. Then there was the more sophisticated type, usually the man who had a car. These offered the girl a lift home; only their plans for getting their ration of passion in the back seat were often thwarted when half a dozen of her friends descended on the car expecting a lift.

Java Writers

Many happily (and unhappily) married couples will tell you where and when they first shifted their spouses. In my own case I shifted my husband-to-be when he was eleven months old, not in Seapoint or the parochial hall, but out of his pram. I arrived several years after my siblings and the pram had already been given away. My next-door neighbour had already grown too big for his, so I became the owner-occupier. We are still together over sixty years later.

Infusions

Java Writers

Infusions

The River
J.G. Lacey

The man reaches the river as the dawn mist is lifting. Like delicate white lace, it furls and twists in a slow ballet along the green water; white smoke, green depth, in a sleeping valley. Early birdsong filters its drowsy melody through folds of meadowland. Quietly, he picks his way among the fronds and green sedges of the riverside and pushes through the hanging screen of willow. There is the old wooden bench, where it has been since his childhood, half sunk in the long grass beside the pool where the mayfly hangs in lemon sunlight.

    He sits on the bench, the exertion of the walk making his clothes prickly and uncomfortable, and once more drags the creased letter from his pocket. He raises his tearful gaze from the words on the page to the bank of the lazily meandering river Suir. His eyes follow the patchwork of emerald fields and the distant brown dots of the grazing cattle all the way to the feet of the Comeragh mountains. Their gentle slopes squat silently in the early sun as they greet the day with the stoic indifference of millennia. Behind him sits the mother mountain, Slievenamon, her green and white streaked top clear in the strengthening light. He remembers a past life. It was on this mountain they had met; in its shadow they had lived and loved but now, like an eternal sentinel, it looms over the final act of their life together. The paper in his hand shivers in the morning breeze, the cold words whispering from the page.

At his feet the water foams over mossy rocks that break here and there through the shallows, and washes the tips of the willows that dip to meet the sparkling surface. Into the silent morning creeps the drone of insects as they whirl in a moving curtain. In a more ancient age, you could almost see the great god Pan come down to the riverbank in the dawn light with his nymphs and fauns. Such fantasies, he knows, are for poetry books and classical studies, happier days when young life passed in a blur of friendship, love and the growing beauty of learning. That's all over now. He begins to read again, the words burning into his brain like sunlight on the water. Mistakes, his mistakes, her mistakes, surely not the end.

Heat seeps slowly into the heavy grasses that enclose the cracked wooden seat, its arms hanging on either side like a tired old man sleeping by the water's edge. As morning turns slowly to noon, the trees, water and mountain fold heavily over his senses, pushing him down to the shadowland where feelings fade. In a dreamlike trance, he rises from the seat, steps forward and stares silently into the dark green depths, where the weed arms open in welcome and the waters whisper sweet oblivion.

As the crimson glow of sunset turns the water to liquid fire, a swan glides regally towards the paper fragment floating in the current. The black marks on it mean nothing; she can't eat it, nor can she read the words that changed everything. With an arch of her long graceful neck, she moves on, serene and uncaring. The water closes silently in her wake, the sun slides behind the watching mountain and the dark shadows rush in.

Infusions

On the mountain, by the black striped darkness of the hazel wood, the woman waits on a rock sunk deep in ancient ground, her eyes sweeping down the silvered slopes. An owl sends a soft boom across the sky and a curlew swoops in the dying light to the reed-hidden nest in the upland scrub. Across the plain and down to the river, the coming night lays its fingers on the landscape and gently rubs the colour from wildwood and fields. She hears the music of distant waters murmuring against the deep chorus of night creatures. There is no sound of human voice, just birdcalls and the plaintive bleating of sheep and cattle sinking slowly to rest after the heat of the day. She stands and stares into the overhanging darkness of the mountain, a silent tear rolling its way down her cheek, a stifled sob intruding briefly on the velvet night. She turns and walks down the slope, until she reaches the lighted square of the window, their refuge for so many years. Her mind whirls. What have we done?

In the scarlet fires of early morning, a warm light creeps down from the peak, caressing the shoulders of Slievenamon. It spreads a silken wave along the floor of the Suir valley and drapes a golden mantle on the ancient stones of Cill Cais and into the low Comeragh hills. The mountain grasses throw splashes of bright green among the blues and purples of the heathers that cover the dawning slopes. Below them, the mighty Suir surges through the open eyes of bridge arches, the soft roaring water plunging onwards in its neverending quest.

In a quiet inlet, where narrow trails of water pause to swirl among the rushes, the faint whisper of a dawn breeze sets the reeds waving gently. The still figure of the man stirs and slowly rises. He looks around at the light beaming life into the still morning and gazes out over the water. He lifts his eyes to the mother mountain and stumbles forward, his heart beating faster, an inner voice urging him onwards.

As sunlight floods the valley, he treads wearily through the deep grass and reaches the foot of the mountain, his breath heaving in his chest and his limbs aching. In the hot breath of noon, he ascends the slope, until he reaches the familiar green place at the forest's edge. In the open doorway she waits and they meet in wordless embrace, the past dissolving in the warmth of the midday sun.

Deep down in the valley, gleaming through the green forest canopy, the river flows on.

Infusions

Java Writers

Infusions

Galway Hookers
Flish McCarthy

Trussed up in their Sunday best,
Blood red, mud brown and maroon black sails
Billowing, the Hookers flew across the Bay
Rounding the buoys set out for the race.
There is a place for everything.

I'd just crested the hill on Dalysfort Road
Where I'd been playing dodge-ems with parked
cars and the 401 Bothar na Tra bus.
There is a place for everything.

My heart was stopped in Shannon
Where daughters boarded planes going elsewhere.
Now I was drawn back to Salthill by these
Racy old girls wearing Galway shawls
And suddenly I knew
There is a place for everyone and just then
I was back in mine.

Java Writers

At Dusk-time
(after Tu Fu)

Black gnats dance
Along the inner pane
Of my open window.

The water below
Is calm and grey in the darkening evening.

The full tide yawns,
draws back white curved lips and
turns to snake toward the far shore
where the lights of Kinvara beckon

And I would have wagered my heart
Was already full when suddenly the
Moon rose above Claddagh,
Looking for all the world like the
Apricots I ate for breakfast.

Infusions

Infusions

Dear Diary, 1965
Duana Sala

25th October
    I just bought you today, was passing by, and saw you in the window, thought it was going to be good for me to share some of my thoughts with something like you, inanimate object, that is going to be my secret, discreet companion, you are never going to judge me, you will be just listening.

30th October
    Well, did not start that well, did I???
    Just bought you and left you there for four days, you are already a bit dusty, but you will have to get used to it, cannot even keep a plant alive cause I often forget watering it.
    Plus, don't really know how to start, have so many things to tell you, and I look at you before going to bed every night, standing there on the bedside table, waiting for me to open my heart to you.
    I feel like I don't trust you yet.
    I feel like I don't trust anybody.
    I need time.

2nd November

I went for a walk today.

The forest drew me to it.

Could see it from far away, from the city, from Trieste; it looked like an enormous colourful rug, looked like a giant could easily enjoy himself walking on it, soft, cosy; red, yellow, green and brown spots everywhere.

Sun was glorious, fresh air was tickling my nose, smell of frost and rotten leaves, I sat under a maple tree, I was surrounded by light, my cold heart wrapped up in a yellow scarf of maple leaves. I closed my eyes and sat there for almost one hour, breathing in the colours, and forgetting about the whole world around me.

4th November

Was reading a book and watching out the window, leaves are falling now, the forest looks like an old rug, used and worn. Burned brown has taken the place of the bright colours that were there just 2 days ago.

Time goes by and everything changes. I cried.

5th November

Felt nostalgic, my neighbours got a piano today, I saw the delivery guys bringing it into the house. It reminded me of a movie I saw with him, *Casablanca*.

A kiss might be just a kiss, but I will never forget it, *"as time goes by"* isn't it true?

10th November

Is very windy outside, the Bora is blowing strongly. I wish it could blow me away as well.

I don't yet know if I am really ready to cope with this, I feel like I want to hide and watch the scene from behind the curtain, I wish I could just be a spectator. I waited for this for so long, and now that it is finally happening I don't know if it's clever.

Infusions

11th November
    I don't like changes. My lips are wet, they taste salty, they taste of happiness, they taste of sadness, they taste of fear and regret and questions not answered. A soup of mixed feelings.

12th November
    13 days left vs. a lifetime of uncertainty and expectations.
    I am finally going to meet my birth mother.
    I have been looking for her since forever.
    I've always known I've been abandoned since I was a kid. The people who brought me up were really good to me and I never lacked for anything.
    The ones I really see like my two mums though, are Silvana and Gisella. My neighbours.
    They taught me what it was crying and laughing. We shared the sound of aeroplanes over Trieste, we shared bombs in 1943, screams, blood and pain. They taught me cross-stitching, baking, cooking; they taught me excitement and suffering, and flirting with the butcher to have some meat for free.
    We shared sunny days and rainy ones where the raindrops mixed with tears. We shared cigarettes, cards games and sunsets; moonlights, dancing, and singing.

16th November
    I TOLD YOU TOO MUCH THE OTHER DAY.
    It felt good, it felt like I was finally able to release my emotions, I felt lighter, thank you.

17th November
    The thing is that I got used to not having my Mum around. I knew she gave me away, I knew she left me with

people who left me with other people, whom are "my" family now.

I got used to not thinking about her, to not asking why she abandoned me, got used to getting no answers back.

Got used to hearing people say that she was only 16 years old when "that" happened, and that she was far too young to keep me, far too poor to earn a living and support me.

I almost forgot, and then he came.

Giulio was his name; we met at a friend's house, love at first sight, disgrace at second.

Damn I still love him so much. But it is something that is never gonna happen.

He is a Carabiniere, damn men in uniform, they are so handsome, and he is a decent fellow, Silvana is mad about him. She says that if her mother Gisella was still alive, if she could have seen me with him, she would have been delighted and so proud.

My family always told me he was not the right one for me, but Silvana has always been a romantic.

Although I hate to admit it, my family was right.

This is not going to be a happy ending.

He cannot marry me, because of that damn abbreviation on my ID that says: N.N. Nomen Nescio, CHILD OF NOBODY. Since he is a soldier, he can't marry a bastard like me. I have not been legally adopted, so on the registry I am an N.N. And he can't marry a N.N.

18th November

I miss him, we decided we could not see each other anymore, he asked to be transferred far away from Trieste. Preferably Roma or Torino. A big city anyway.

I can't cope with the pain I feel in my heart. But I want to meet my mother.

At least all this pain will bring something into my life, it will bring answers, it will bring certainty.

Infusions

As soon as I broke up with Giulio I started my research. It was like I was trying to fill the gap left by him. It was not easy. My family never got to know who my real mother was. They preferred not to ask. Reluctantly they told me who the people were who brought me into their house.

They asked me why I wanted to know, they could not understand. They still can't.

Those people were not even living in Trieste anymore, I had to write letters, and patiently wait for their answer, not sure if I would ever get one.

When the letter arrived I had goose bumps, and I had to leave it there for days, on the bedside table, where I now put you.

When I opened it and I read it, I spoiled it with tears, trying not to cry and to preserve the letter as intact as possible, so that I could still read the address and most importantly the name of my mother: Clara.

20th November

5 days to go, what will I say?

I wrote her a letter almost two weeks ago, explaining briefly who I was.

Who I was. It sounded strange, awkward: *Hi I'm very pleased to meet you, I'm your daughter.*

I thought it was going to be difficult, life taught me that nothing is easy, that you have to fight for everything, that you don't deserve happiness if you are not ready to fight for it. Everyone deserves happiness; nobody should have to fight for it.

It surprised me how quickly the answer came. Her handwriting was so neat and gorgeous, very feminine, but the letter was so brief, she told me to meet her in Marina Julia.

21ᵗʰ November

I'm going crazy. Too many things running through my head. I wish I could tell her everything I want, but am afraid that the words won't come when I'm there.

I'll write them all here, in a letter, if I decide not to go, if I turn back when I see her. If tears are going to freeze my lips and throat, at least I will have it all written down.

"Hi Clara, Hi Mum.

I never felt like calling Sior Enzo and Siora Maria mother and father, but I have to say that I was not fair to them, cause they gave me everything they could.

They loved me, respected me, fed me and encouraged me like they did with their own kids. But I feel like calling YOU mum.

I've always known you were out there, they never lied to me, I knew I had a mother, I knew you were young, I knew you did not want to leave me, but had to.

I don't blame you mum. To be honest, I have to say, that there have been moments that I totally forgot about you, I just got on with my life, I assumed it was normal not to know my real mother, I assumed it was safe, wise, I assumed that it was how my life was going to be, I took for granted that my life was uncertain, messed up, built up on false expectations. Like the one of seeing you walking through my door, finally looking for me.

I thought that if you were not looking for me, neither should I.

And it hurt.

Then something changed, I met a man, Giulio, he is a Carabiniere, we fell in love, but life cheated us. He cannot marry me, cause I am a child of nobody. But I am your child Clara, am I not?

Giulio and I are not together anymore, and I feel now so close to you, like I have never been before to anybody in my entire life. Why is that? Is it magic? I feel the bond. I feel like it is the only real thing I have left."

26th November

I met my mother. She looks so fragile, she is tiny and pale, she reminds me of the porcelain doll that Silvana keeps in her bedroom. She has blue eyes, sad eyes, they were filled with tears when she saw me in Marina Julia and instinctively recognized me. We did not have to say anything. We just hugged.

Life is peculiar. I don't know if the bond I feel is because she is my mother, or because the stories of our lives are so similar. She said my father looked like one of those statues you see on the books, he came with the waves, he did not speak Italian, but his heart spoke for him.

They met on the shore, and my mother gave him the most precious present of all, she gave him love.

And my mum kept living there, close to the sea and to the waves, listening to their lapping and splashing, like a shell hiding a pearl within, hoping that the coming tide would one day bring him back to her.

But the waves never got to rock him with their lullaby, because soon after making love to my mum, the war took his life away. *"You were my jewel, I was just 16 years old, I could not keep that gift,"* she kept repeating.

20th December

I'm visiting my mother every week, I'm sharing every single emotion with her, I feel like we have to compensate all the time spent apart. I love listening to her stories, and love hearing about my father, about his thick blond hair and blue eyes. I can trust. I can trust again.

I've never seen Giulio again. I've heard he is living in Roma now, and that's all.

Dear Diary, my name is Claudia.

Java Writers

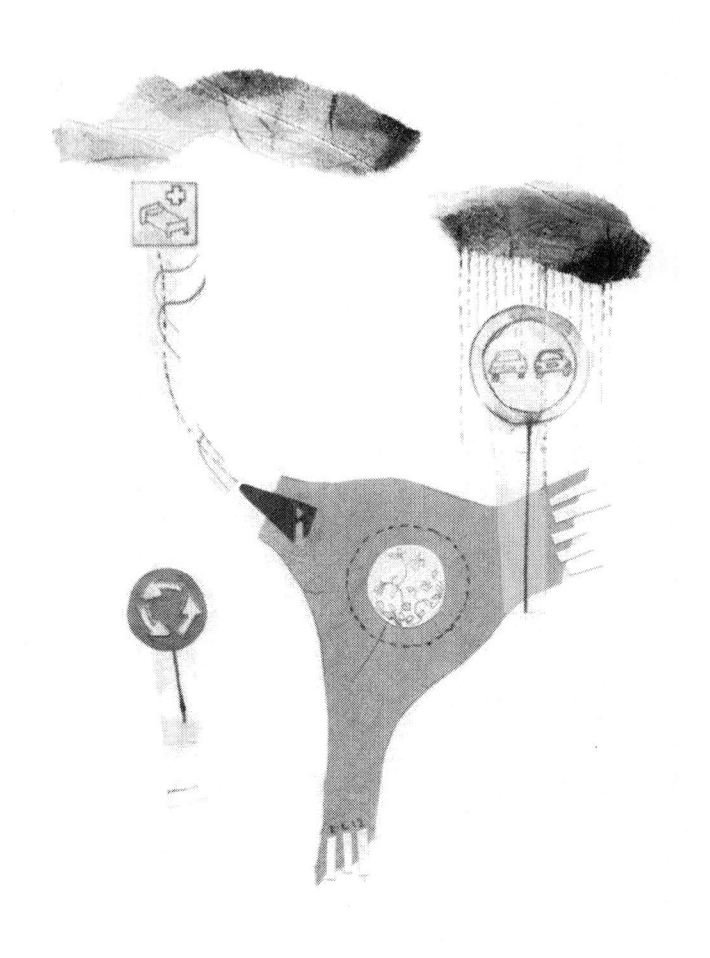

Karma
Margaret Brady

Caroline drummed her fingers on the steering wheel of her Mini Cooper and rolled her eyes. God she hated this shift with a passion. Getting in for nine in the morning was a pain in the neck. Such a waste of time and effort and petrol.

It had taken less than fifteen minutes to get the fifteen kilometres from her house to the start of this road and a further fifteen minutes, so far, to inch her way along its half a kilometre length. Rush hour had got to be the most infuriating and futile hour of anyone's day. No wonder there are so many instances of road-rage she thought as she felt herself getting agitated.

She took some calming deep breaths and checked her watch again. It was now a quarter to nine and there were still eleven cars in front of her in the queue for the roundabout. She started to worry that she wouldn't actually make it in on time. The worst bit was, since she crested the hill, she could see her destination. She could walk it in two minutes but she was beginning to doubt she could drive it in fifteen.

"Why does everything in this stupid country have to start at nine? Could the powers that be not stagger the start of the work day so that the whole bloody country is not on the roads at the same time?"

She watched a group of school children, laughing and joking and pushing and shoving each other as they sauntered past her. She timed them until they reached the car park she so badly wanted to be in. Just over two minutes and they weren't exactly rushing. The single line of traffic continued to inch closer to the roundabout as one by one the cars in front of her made it on to the main road. She moved again, just one car length.

"Oh, for God's sake," she snapped. "Get a bloody move on."

She fiddled with the radio hoping to pick up a good song to take her mind off the fleeting time and her rising blood pressure. Three channels in a row were on an ad break, where someone, cheerful to the point of mania, was trying to sell her something she didn't really need. Another was giving out a traffic report.

"Traffic is slow this morning, with long delays on all the roundabouts," said the newsreader in an overly cheerful voice. Probably because he wasn't the one of the unfortunates stuck in a stupid traffic jam.

"No bloody kidding, Einstein, tell me something I don't know!" she snapped at him before changing channel again.

Next up was a DJ, obviously in love with the sound of his own voice, prattling on and on about what he did and who he saw at various nightclubs at the weekend. "I mean, who cares? Right?" It did nothing to calm her frustration. No one was playing music, she noted. "Does nobody play music anymore?" she wondered as she stabbed the pre-sets before she settled on iRadio. "In New York…" she sang along in her best American accent. When Jay-Z finished singing *Empire State of Mind* and the ads came on she flicked again and inched forward another car length.

"God, I hate this shift," she moaned. "Thank God I've only got three more days left of this before I'm back on the 6:00 shift. I'd go mental if I had to do this forty-five weeks of the year. Brilliant. Now I'm talking to myself. First sign of madness. Going mental already and it's only been a quarter of an hour."

She glanced around to see had anyone noticed. Nobody had. No one cared what she was up to in her own little cocoon. The other drivers she could see had the slack face and the vacant stare of an automaton as they shuffled forward on autopilot.

"What do I care anyway, if anyone bothers to look at me they'll just assume I'm on a hands-free set." Her mind wandered off and she thought about what she could be doing right now. Normally, at this time, she'd be eating breakfast. "I'd murder a coffee just about now."

Ollie Turner was on Galway Bay FM doing his Big Breakfast Smoothie as she moved the car forward without being aware of her actions. "This is for everyone stuck in traffic this morning – 'Hey! You! Get offa my cloud'!"

"Oooh! I haven't heard this song - in - forever!" She turned up the volume and sang along with The Rolling Stones and thought that she really must give her dad a ring. She had moved three car lengths closer to the roundabout without even noticing.

A white Mitsubishi was right alongside her with its engine roaring. It was doing at least eighty kph down the other side of the road in the wrong direction. It seemed to her to have come out of nowhere and gave her such a fright she stalled the car. She recoiled in her seat and watched in horror, hoping and praying that nothing was turning off the roundabout against him expecting their side of the road to be clear. They wouldn't stand a chance.

Breaks screeching, he cut aggressively across the car at the top of the queue and out onto the main road. The driver in the first car, not expecting to be overtaken while turning onto a roundabout, had to break hard to avoid a collision. The car behind him nearly ran up the back of him. The bloody moron had no idea of the chaos he could have left in his wake.

"MORON!" Her heart pounded. "You'll end up killing somebody!"

She took some slow deep breaths to calm her nerves, She sat for a few seconds with her hand on the key, before she turned it and re-started the car. Her heartbeat slowly returned to normal as she continued her forward shuffle. Finally she got across the roundabout and had to run through the car park to make it into work on time.

On Tuesday morning Caroline left her house five minutes earlier in the hope of getting to the roundabout before the major traffic build up. As she patiently queued for the turnoff at the roundabout she kept checking in her mirrors. After the fright she got yesterday she didn't want to be taken unawares again. When she was about five cars from the top she thought perhaps yesterday was an exception, but no, there was "Moron" again. On the wrong side of the road, coming up fast. He passed so close to her car this time that it rocked on its suspension. The car in front of her jerked to a stop and its driver leaned on his horn and stuck his head out the window, shaking his fist after "Moron", bellowing "Yeh Gobshite yeh!"

"Moron" swerved into the top of the line again and was gone. She recited his reg. number until she had it scribbled down on the back of an envelope with a pencil she fished out of the side pocket. A few people were still beeping their horns after him in shock and annoyance. Even though she had been half expecting it, she was still unsettled. If everyone drove like that we could halve the population within a year, she thought. That would solve the unemployment crisis and the rush hour traffic jams in one fell swoop. When she got into work she rang the police.

Infusions

On Wednesday morning, as she joined the end of the queue for the roundabout, she looked for the traffic cop with the speed camera she hoped would be there. No sign. They would probably be closer to the junction anyway. After giving them all the details yesterday she really hoped there might be one somewhere. After all, not only was what he had done illegal but it was also extremely dangerous. Too many people were killed and injured on the roads by morons like this one. She had no intention of being one of them.

    She looked in her mirrors again and could see a white car about six cars behind her. Was that him, behaving himself for once? She could hear someone behind her revving their engine. A brief glance in her mirror showed her the white car edging out of the lane getting ready for the run down the wrong side. Someone had to do something. She waited until he was alongside her and blew her horn as he passed by. He was going too fast for her to get a good look at him but she could make out he was in his late teens or early twenties.

    She shifted around in her seat and looked at the driver behind her. The people in the car were visibly shocked and the driver shook her head making a gesture with her index finger up against her temple suggesting "Moron" was a complete and utter nutter. Not even her favourite song, Candi Staton's *Young Hearts Run Free* could settle her.

    "Why is there never a cop when you need one?"

    On the final morning of her nine o'clock start as Caroline edged slowly up to the roundabout she hoped the police would be there. Once again she was disappointed. She heard him coming before she saw him. She checked in her mirrors to confirm it was "Moron". Yep. It was him alright. Happily driving in his own private lane. Oblivious to all the dangers he posed to himself and others. She readied herself to beep at him again when he passed. As she pressed the horn, he slowed right down to a crawl. This time she was able to get a really good look at him as he passed her. He was laughing at her as he gave her the middle finger. Then he blew her a cheeky kiss before he sped right back up and cut sharply into the traffic in front. "Eejit! What a total plonker."

On Friday morning Caroline left her house at half past five. By the time Queen finished singing *Bohemian Rhapsody* she was negotiating the empty roundabout. She checked in her mirrors to see if "Moron" was there. She knew it was about three hours before his usual time so she doubted he would be, but you never know. Thankfully he wasn't. By ten to she was parked up, clocked in and sitting behind her desk going through her "in" tray, catching up on her paperwork.

"We were spoiled for the last few days, Orla, with the nice weather."

"Yeah, back to the usual rain today. We'll probably get really busy shortly."

"People usually take it easier in the rain."

"Most people do. There are still some loonies out there though."

"Tell me about it. For the last few mornings I've been seeing this guy in a white Mitsubishi pulling some very dodgy manoeuvres."

"Some young fellas think they're immortal. Then they're really surprised to discover they're not."

"Too true. As we well know."

"Bet you anything we're flat out by nine."

"Ok. It's just a little past eight now. So I'm going to bow to your sixth sense about these things, take full advantage of the lull and have my breakfast break now. Just in case."

Caroline was sitting in the canteen finishing her second hot buttered scone and a cup of tea when her pager went off. She checked it. "RTA" it read. She drained the last drop of tea as she stood up and popped the little bit of extra crunchy crust she was saving till last into her mouth.

"God Orla, I love the early start. It's so civilised. This time yesterday I was sitting in traffic at the roundabout nearly ripping my hair out," said Caroline as she walked back in, pulling on her white coat. 'What have we got?'

"As predicted and right on time. First of this morning's rush hour fender benders," said Orla as she handed the chart to Caroline. "I know what you mean, I hate that bloody roundabout too. An asshole cut me up there last week. Nearly ploughed right into me. I was still shaking when I got in here."

"That's where I saw 'Moron', the Mitsubishi guy, at that roundabout," said Caroline as she tapped the chart and added, "Where's the RTA?"

"Curtain one, Doctor. Car and truck. Head on. Truck driver's fine, just suffering from shock. The car driver wasn't as lucky. You've got him. The paramedics suspect a concussion, a probable dislocated shoulder and he'll need stitches in a head wound," Orla said as she checked her chart for the relevant details. "The car that cut me up was white too, I don't know what make though. There's not that many white ones. Maybe it was the same guy."

"Maybe," said Caroline and she glanced through the chart as she pulled back the curtain.

"Good morning, I'm Doctor Caroline O'Neill, I'll be looking after…"

She looked up, smiling, to make eye contact with the patient but she didn't finish her sentence. Her eyes widened and her mouth gaped open. All she could do was stare at the patient in disbelief. There he lay, bloodied and battered but unmistakably …

"Moron!"

"Cooper-woman?"

Ollie Turner nattered away on the radio in the background. "Here's one from the archives for all you aging hippies out there. The year was 1970… the late, the great, John Lennon and *Instant Karma!*"

"Instant Karma's going to get you…" sang Lennon. "Gonna knock you right on the head…"

Infusions

Infusions

A Funny Thing
Bern Butler

Elaine stopped. To her right was a small graveyard, which she didn't remember being there before. She looked back along the narrow path she had come. There was something different. Where was the white bench in front of the convent door? Where was the convent? She looked ahead. Where was the little flower bed with the statue of the kneeling St. Bernadette?

This was a different path entirely, she realised, to the shortcut she normally took, to get from the car park to the bank. How had that happened? She looked up and down the path again, puzzled. There must be two gates, she thought, and she had taken the wrong one in her distraction. It's all this stuff going on with Greg and me, she thought, making me go a bit funny.

Elaine looked in more closely at the plot. There were about twenty white wrought-iron crosses, scattered, almost randomly, in the grass. Humble, simple, straight forward crosses about a foot high, with the grass tickling their stems. A tall black cross stood in the middle towering over the little ones. An arc of cool evergreens, like footmen, stood silently around the perimeter.

This was where they buried the nuns from the convent, she surmised. The idea, of a particular graveyard for nuns, had never crossed her mind before. She imagined an old nun in the convent, dying in her bed, surrounded by candles and praying nuns. It felt like an odd thought and for some reason reminded her of a scene from a story about Chekhov. At the same time, she wished, despite everything, that Greg was here with her, that they were standing at the railing looking in, at the poignant little graveyard, together.

She looked in more closely at the black cross. On the cross it said, "Reverend Mother Beningnus." My God, Elaine thought, because she was a reverend mother, she gets a bigger cross than the rest of them. This makes a mockery of it all, she thought, and her heart went out to the dead nuns in their graves. The only information on their crosses was a name: Sr. Nunciata, Sr. Joseph, Sr. Clare and so on, along with their dates of birth and death - separated by a small dash, which, it struck Elaine, summed up a life. Nuns, like every other living thing, come into being then die, she thought, a play of plus and minus, where the curtains are raised and dropped at the same time. A cancelled performance, where, nonetheless, the show must go on.

A riddle.

Her eye was caught by a blackbird, there, by the railing, stabbing at a slug curled in the throes of dying; here, at her feet, the grey mop of a dandelion-head collapsed into seed, behind her, in the church car-park, a hearse was gliding to a halt, and the big hand on the white clock face was about to strike the hour. Elsewhere, she imagined: by the sea, a white wave crashing onto the promenade, and in a green field somewhere, a skinny foal rising shakily to its feet, while behind the corrugated shed, a farmer was cocking his rifle at the circling crows. In the kitchen, each morning, a heap of flies could be found, lying, dead, below the light bulb – and here now, the church bells, clamouring for attention, were clanging noon.

    Here now, she stood listening to them - a soul who had lost her way, looking in at a nun's graveyard, while all about her the world played on in a teeming nonsense.

    Nothing makes any sense, she thought.

    There stood the knowing, dumb evergreens.

    Here were the quiet nuns in their graves.

    Elaine blessed herself, then made her way back, the way she had come, wanting to get home quickly, to tell Greg about her curious little find.

When she got home, Greg was standing at the cooker stirring a pot of pasta. Steam billowed out and around the kitchen. Elaine went to him and kissed his cheek. She took the spoon out of his hand and turned on the fan over the cooker. Greg sat back at his chair by the table where his laptop sat.

    "How was your day?" she asked, stirring.

    "Same-o, same-o," he said.

    "Any luck?" she asked.

    "No," he said.

    Elaine said nothing. Greg said nothing.

    "What's with the pasta?" asked Elaine, still stirring.

    "What?" said Greg. Elaine turned around.

    "The pasta. What's with the pasta?" she said again. Greg looked blankly at her. Elaine turned back to the pot. There was a silence. Elaine heard Greg tap on the keys of the laptop. She breathed out with the steam.

    "I saw a funny thing," she began.

    "Oh yea," said Greg.

    "Yea," said Elaine. She took a breath in. "I was taking the shortcut from the car park to the bank, you know the one," she said, "through the convent and then I realised I had gone the wrong way."

    "Oh yea?" said Greg.

"Yea, I don't know how I did it." Elaine stopped. She suddenly felt like crying. "I think," she said, turning around, "that I was very distracted." Greg was staring at something on the screen. "You know," she continued, "I bought some credit for my phone today and when I got outside the shop I threw it in the bin and when I realised, I went back to the shop –" she paused, willing Greg to look up at her, but he didn't.

She took a breath and went on, "and the shop assistant had to unlock the bin. Did you know they had locks for bins?" Greg was still staring at the screen. "And then we couldn't find it. I think the shop assistant, took it, or something..." she trailed off.

"Hard to get good help these days," said Greg after a pause, and with his hand clicking on the computer's mouse.

Elaine looked at him. The shoulders on him, she thought, that lip hanging like a fish's. This uselessness. She turned back to the pasta. A moment later, Greg said,

"What about the funny thing?" Elaine didn't answer. Greg prompted. "You said you saw something funny."

"It wasn't funny, like that," Elaine said, and she tossed the wooden spoon down on to the chopping board.

"No – go on," said Greg. "What was it?" He pushed the laptop away from him. He looked up at her. "Tell me."

"It was nothing," Elaine said.

"Great," said Greg, "nothing," and he sighed. Elaine turned off the cooking ring and the overhead fan. A silence like toxic smoke invaded the kitchen.

"What's the matter?" Greg asked quickly.

"Nothing," Elaine said.

"Oh, is that all?" said Greg. He snapped the laptop shut.

Elaine leant back against the countertop and looked at the floor. Greg folded his arms across his chest.

"You never listen," said Elaine. Greg sighed and shook his head. "Sorry for the cliché," Elaine added, "I know you hate clichés. But it's true. You never listen." She paused. "Sorry for being a cliché," she said.

"I listen," Greg said. He was massaging a drop of water into the tablecloth with his fingertip.

"No," said Elaine, "you don't. I was talking to you. I was trying to tell you something."

"I was listening," he said.

"You weren't," said Elaine

"You said you saw a funny thing. That's what you said. I heard you. I was listening. I wanted to know what was the funny thing was."

"Yes," said Elaine "and I wanted to tell you. I wanted to tell you all about it. You were the first person I thought of," and then added, "when I saw it," and a nervous laugh, like a sudden bird from a hedge, flew out of her mouth. Greg didn't smile.

"What was the funny thing?" he said.

"Stop calling it that," Elaine said. She didn't really know what she was going to say. "We haven't spoken-" her voice gave way. She pressed the heels of her hands onto the worktop and tried again. "We haven't spoken for days," she went on, "I really wanted to tell you about the nuns. I missed you or something. I wished you were there. And then when I started telling you, you were just tapping on that bloody thing," she nodded to the keyboard, "as if I didn't matter. As if we didn't matter." She paused.

"Nuns?" said Greg, "but you didn't say anything about nuns."

"Oh whatever," said Elaine "nuns, birds, dandelions. It doesn't matter," and she folded her arms across her chest.

"You sound like some long-suffering kind of martyr," said Greg. "But, it's not just you that's trying, you know. It's not just you, right?" he said, and looked at her. "I was trying too. But see you, yea? Straight away, just in the door, you go 'What's with the pasta?'" He waved an arm in the air. "What do you think I am?" He raised his voice. "You actually thought I was cooking just plain pasta, didn't you? 'How like a stupid man,' I bet you were thinking." Elaine looked at the ground. "You were, weren't you?"

Greg stood up and went to the fridge. He took out a carton of cream and some smoked salmon.

"Sorry to disappoint you," he said, and he tossed them onto the table.

"And oh yea," he said and he went back and opened the fridge door. He took a bowl of salad and placed it on the table too. "Here's one I made earlier," he said. "Hungry?"

Elaine shook her head.

"No, me neither," he said.

Greg sat back down at the table. Elaine started to cry. Greg put his head into his hands. After a few moments Elaine said,

"It's just that I had come in from work and even though we hadn't been talking, I wanted to try."

"Leave it," said Greg.

"I really wanted to tell you about what I saw," said Elaine. Greg didn't answer. Elaine was silent for a moment.

"No," she said then, "I won't! I won't leave it. I won't leave it just because you say so." She was looking at him but he wouldn't look up. "We're always leaving it. That's the problem. We never talk about anything." She looked at Greg with his head in his hands. "Greg?" she said.

"Leave me alone," he said.

"Oh, aren't you all day, every day, on your bloody own," she said. "What on earth is wrong with you?"

Greg raised his head slowly and stared at her.

"Ah ha," he said nodding his head, "the nub of the problem. We finally get to what's really bothering Elaine." He pushed back the chair noisily. "Fuck this for a picnic," he said and took his coat off the back of the chair.

Through the front window Elaine saw him get into his car and when she stopped looking, she heard the tyres crunch on the gravel as he took off.

Infusions

    She sat at the table. Did I just do that, she wondered? Was it me, who made that happen?

Night let itself unobtrusively into the kitchen. On the cooker, the pasta congealed and became grey and discoloured. Elaine sat on in the dusk, wrestling. If only I could feel the whole thing, complete for an instant, she thought, if I could grasp the tail of that elusive animal, everything would be different, but it is like trying to see around a corner, or imagine the face of a loved one in your head.
    I never got to tell him about the nuns, she thought. Maybe, when he gets back. And Elaine sat for a long time at the table, puzzling over, how the world kept turning and how funny things kept happening, over and over, again.
    Nothing makes any sense, she thought.

Java Writers

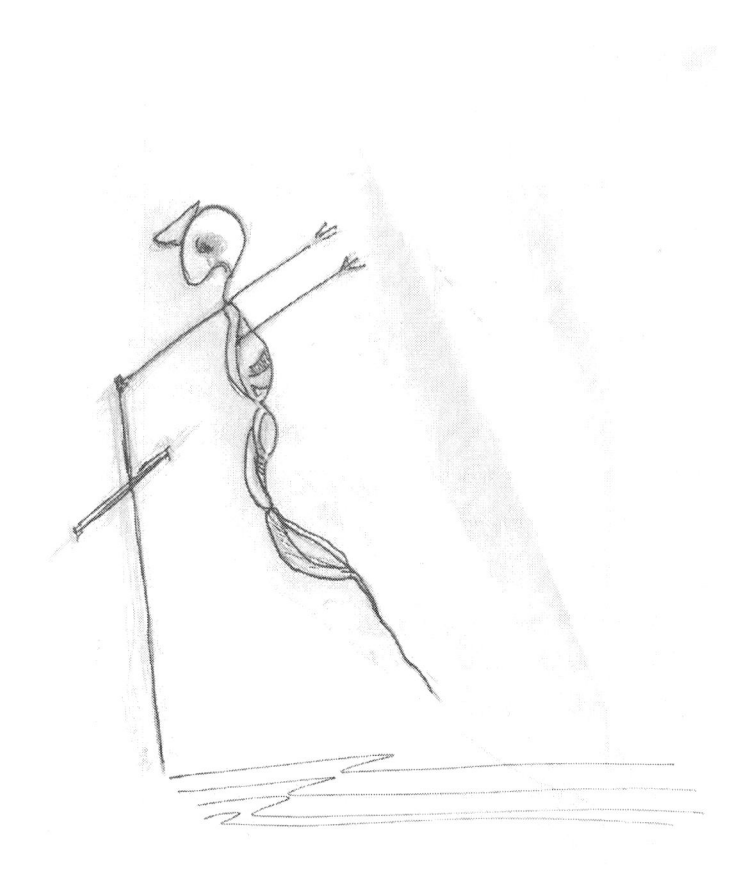

Infusions

Te Quiero
Philipa Maguire

We run like wild cats, zigzagging our way through the streaming shadows of the bin lined streets of Soho, our feet kicking the water, which lines every crevice of the cobbled streets. Breathing in the cold air, we stop, look at each other and run for our lives, to the old blue laundry trolley, which stands where we had left it parked, waiting.

"You win," he says.

I nod.

Taking out his tobacco stash he rolls two thin fags. We stand there amidst the prostitutes and vomit, in the quiet of the Sunday morning, inhaling deeply into our young lungs. We look. Taking a last drag we dare each other, watching every movement we run to the back of the trolley, pushing, heaving, swinging it up the hill as it groans, rattles and shudders, wrenching its grip on every dip in the street. We glance eagerly as we feel the excitement building. Then Alfredo gives the thumbs up. At that moment, we push with all our might as we both hold on to either side. We take off down the bumpy road, daring each other to swing it harder and harder.

Java Writers

The rattle, screech, and hum of the trolley reverberates in the narrow streets, as we clatter into dustbins, upsetting the contents and the cold ravens who fly at us, flapping and squawking.

Faster faster our hearts sing. Swinging out to far and hitting a bump, I fall off which upsets everything. Rolling off the ground, all I can see is this rickety old trolley taking on a life on its own, hurtling down the street. Alfredo is clinging for all his life, his long skinny body, a black fly trapped, as it uproots on top of him, crash.

The crack of the trolley hitting the wall as the dirty sheets from the hostel lurch out, like a blanket they cover the wet ground. The silence echoes through me. Only my heart's thumping. Running, with all my might I make it to the trolley, which seems to have eaten up Alfredo. Yanking the trolley, I keep repeating to myself please don't be dead, please don't be dead, like a mantra it rolls and rolls in my mind. Please don't be dead, don't be dead and through my fear steamed eyes I find him.

His long narrow face looks blue, his eyes shut, body still.

I run my hands over his face.

"Are you dead?" I whisper silently as the tears roll down my face. "Are you dead?"

He doesn't move. I feel his hair, its long dark coils wrapping my hand. Touching it, praying, while he just lies there. I start to shake him, weeping, "wake up, wake up, don't die," leaning over and listening to his heart. It beats!

"Stop," he breathes, "you are hurting."

Slowly he moves, turning his young skinny body with delicate movements.

"You are not dead," I say aloud, shuddering with fright as the croaking words seem to squeak along the battered street screaming in the silence.

"You cry that for me?" His face lighting up with joy and as I help him up, he grasps, turns and kisses me.

Infusions

"No one, ever cries for me," he whispers enclosing me in his long thin arms and among the upturned trolley, dirty sheets, and rain I find someone whom I can love.

We start to pick up the sheets, one hand held tight, we swing together like some arc sheet-grabbing monster moving in union. He suddenly grabs me and throws the sheets in the air, spinning me over his shoulder.

"She speaks, she speaks, she speaks!"

Putting me down he looked deeply into my eyes, "you speak, you speak, you cry for me. Oh man."

He starts to do a crazy walk, twisting and jumping.

"She speaks, cries for me. I am the man." And the more he contorts himself the more he captures me.

Among the tears I hear a strange sound, I am laughing. We both laugh in wonder, amazement, poking each other, touching, throwing sheets in the air. Dancing we circle the cobbled street, our place of wonder, eyes questioning, seeking deeper parts of each other. Sharing a fag, sitting on the wet street.

"Why no speak? English?"

I just hang my head whispering "Irish, don't tell, don't tell, they will find me if I speak."

"I will tell," he cries. "Yes, I tell," he grabs me. "You now Maria from Barcelona, have no voice." Yes I am Maria. I am Spanish and it is great.

"Hi dumm-y, what does dummy do today?" sings scab face as she circles the table, kicking me when she gets the chance. "Can dumm-y talk, can dumm-y walk?" She laughs.

I sit still.

"No point talking to the dummy, she is just a dumm-y. Dummy do what dummy does."

I don't look at the voice, I know who she is, pins in mattresses, knife blade pushing up from the lower bunk.

She can't touch me, pain doesn't bother me. Do your worst is what I think.

But Maria gets up smiling and punches her.

This is my last warning so I am out. I don't mind and Maria just giggles.

"You mad Spanish girl," is all he says when he finds me crouching in a doorway. "Come."

Arms tight, we walk, stop, hugging each other. By the river we listen to the water, gushing flowing living.

"It flows all the way home, you come home, one day.

"Here I have a present," and we run to his Bridge. "See she is beautiful," he raises his hands up, "she is wonderful. All the lights on this Bridge I give you." We hang over the side watching the reflections of the lights swaying, moving, in and out patterns of time. "Some day I build a bridge like this. Maria's bridge."

The light seeps through the caked Georgian window of our Camberwell Grove squat. It struggles to bounce off the black painted, peeling room. Listening rats scuttle overhead to Alfredo's soothing snores. I hug myself. A whole room to ourselves, I can't believe it. It is huge. We have been in a few squats: most of them, you have to outmanoeuvre the Punks, Skinheads or the Peckham Boys long enough to cross the vast concrete basins. Always dodging, sometimes crawling, sneaking, being invisible behind wheels, cars, bins, walls, anything that offers camouflage. Maria is fearless; she has a knife and will use it. Lying on the floor with an assortment of sleeping bags, rugs, clothes strewn across us, we stay warm, engrossed, happy.

I am going to Spain, to Pamplona .We are going to run with the bulls, throw tomatoes in Valencia. Leaning over, touching him, the wonder of him, the joy of him, the fun of him, my heart quivers every time I see him, I am his Maria. He is my life.

Infusions

I never talk. Alfredo looks at me sometimes, wondering, but he never gives away my secret. Soon everyone accepts Maria as she is, my dark Celtic looks becoming Spanish.

We have spent the months in the deep caverns of the London Underground, sometimes begging, most times dancing, shaking a tambourine, groups of us hang, till we are moved. It seems to me the people all march to a tune that I never heard. Shoes, boots, toes, clip-clop of feet, feet everywhere when you're sitting. Sometimes people throw money at us, most times not. We borrow, steal, jump on buses, run for our lives. We are part of a whole network of invisible people, who appear out of nowhere. We all know where to get free food, free clothes, cash jobs. We party in warehouses, squats; we dance to the new music. Mad, mayhem we rock till dawn comes or the pigs. It is so cool. Alfredo smiling, running, showing, singing, laughing; most nights we go to the bridge in homage to its beauty. There we weave our dreams.

That night we leave another warehouse party where Alfredo knows the DJ. We have both been working, partying. We have money and are both nicely happy, the alcohol highlighting my love for him.

We run to our bridge. We both jump up on the rails, balancing hands out, daring each other, one following the other, tottering, messing, pretending to jump in, faking, lurching, then diving, goading each other till one of us gives up, jumps down, safe. The glittering lights beaming our shadows everywhere, as we chase each other up and down the bridge. Our young bodies willows in the breeze as we fly together in our flight for freedom. The warm smell of his leather jacket over both our shoulders, as we snuggle together for our ritual fag. The dawn rises cold and we sit there, keeping warm with the smoke in our lungs, he whispers to me in Spanish.

Java Writers

I hang on to everything he says. I love him so much that I want to talk, I need to talk but I am afraid to talk. He loves me this way. If I talk I will ruin it. He will hate me. I never could get the words to work for me. Always saying the wrong thing, then the guillotine.

The intensity of his kiss hits me. I cling to him. Putting his jacket over me, suddenly he runs from me, and I start laughing, teasing, I run after him, and we dart right then left over the bridge.

He bounces up on the rails again, scrambling, I laugh. One foot in front of the other, hands out, balancing - *see I can fly!* - I watch him fake jumping.

Te quiero (I love you), the words start bubbling up in me. Rising, heaving, lodging on my vocal cords. I start spluttering, mouthing, and as they come roaring out of my mouth, he jerks balancing and just slips away off the bridge. In that split second his life, ingrained, flies into the dirty running water screaming.

I try to jump in after him. I stand on the rail and try and try to jump but it is like some vast sticky stuff has captured my legs, holds me there static. I run from side to side, where are you? I sit squatting, hunkered down, begging a God that has never heard, to give him back. The black waters of the river just go on and on, I look and look into the murky mists but nothing, nothing.

I sit there forever, waiting for him, steeped in black horror.

Wrapping myself in his jacket, smelling his warmth, hollow, lost, unable to follow. I can't, I can't follow him. I can't love him. I don't love him.

For I know as I have always known that they are right, no good would come to me, I was the devil, destroying all that I touch, evil penetrating everything.

The loathing never leaves me. I smell her now, her, she who takes everything away. The deep hatred for her sears

Infusions

through me. Scar-scraped arms swinging, moving, she touches him he dies.

The police are looking for me. Run I run. Hitching. Lorries pulling over. Taking they take. Smiling touch me He dies.

Somewhere on the leaving, a memory, a voice maybe school talking about Allihies in County Cork where the sea is so wild and free. Yes, free finally free of her and me.

"Do you want a lift or what?" booms the thick Cork voice. Nodding, I have fallen asleep on the wet curb, soaked, dirty, uncaring, my sign for Allihies planted by my bag.

"Put your stuff in the back, there, don't mind the mongrel, he's only an old flee bitten warrior."

I don't care about the dog, a part of me hopes the large animal will bite me and then I'd die.

It will be all over, this living, horrible living. I am as black as I have ever been, I have no reason to live and I am not looking for one. I just want the release to death, away from the living, the happy, the sane. Smiling yes. It will be soon, so soon in the sea in Allihies.

"Be careful where you put your feet, she's got a little bit of rust."

I look down at the floor and see what he means.

"Where are you from?"

I point to my throat, shaking my head.

"Jesus you poor thing, the mother has a great cure for that. Fuck listen to this, like is this the best or what? Rory is the man. Yea, he's on fire." As the music booms out he starts to laugh, his long red hair shaking with him.

Dipping into my pockets I pull out tobacco and papers, pointing at them and at him.

"You're a girl after my own heart."

The smoke draws into our lungs and leaves us in our own world. My clothes start steaming.

Java Writers

"Fuck are you wet or what?" he roars over the sounds of Rory Gallagher. "That Jinx album, boy it rocks. I'm a fisherman, like, fishing out of Castletownbere. Me, like, with the grandfather, boy. Was in Cork for a party. Man it was a monster, a fucking monster. Great weed. Did you ever try those fucking magic mushrooms? Natural or what."

I must have fallen asleep in the warmth of the car.

"Do you think she'll be alright or what? Like, I'm sorry, I only gave her a lift, now I leave you with all this trouble." As my eyes come into focus I can see two people at the end of the bed.

Blinking I try to move but cannot.

"The poor thing is exhausted, she's no trouble. You don't be worrying, it's your special nature, Rory," she says, turning toward him smiling. "You've a kind heart, sure how could you leave the poor creature by the side of the road." She touches his face with her hand. "Go, keep a sharp eye out. Don't let himself do too much."

She helps me sit, feeds me soup, tells me stories. She moves around me like an Angel. Gently soothing, caring for me in a way that I have never known. When I am well enough I sit in the warm, snug kitchen and watch her bake. She sings, to welcome the day, no matter what it brings her. Her kitchen is her heart: warm, bright yellow room with rays of sunshine bouncing from window to window. It is full of colours; her paintings hang on every wall, pieces of shells washed by the sea, wild flowers at dawn, the most compelling a stormy black seascape.

One day she sits me down at the table full of wonderful smells, the range warm against the wind.

"I don't want you to be leaving, not for a while, it's lovely having you here. There is something about you that fills my heart." She holds my hands over the table. "I know, stay for a while. God has sent you to me. I have but one son, my beautiful daughter was taken when she was young, now God has sent you." Tears run down her serene face. "I know you have troubles, your eyes speak of suffering. Know that I am here, I will help you carry your burden." Coming over to me she gives me a hug, which I cannot accept. "Someday when you are ready, you will talk," she whispers into my ear. "Now," wiping her face, "we must get ready for the men, help me daughter."

The sun rises every day. It's just sometimes hidden by the clouds. I start to believe her but I am tired, so tired, I can only do the basic things for myself. Most of the time I spend in the kitchen looking out at the sea, or curled up in granddad's old chair beside the range. She is always there when I wake up screaming. Holding, soothing, hugging till the pain subsides. During the week the house is ours, filled with music, chat, and stories. The work is done in a gentle rhythm. The weekends are full of men and fish.

Soon I am baking with her, following her every move. She teaches me so much.

Her laugh as she places the brush in my hand, "don't be afraid, any daughter of mine can paint," and I do. She starts to write letters to me, every night she leaves one on my bed. Soon I am writing back to her. At first she wants to know my name, I tell her I have none so we settle on daughter. She writes about everything, things I have never heard of, soon we spend the evenings writing to each other. Her joy in all that she does rubs off on me. Every day I vow to go and every day I stay. The best thing ever is that I am someone's daughter. She loves me. She really does. Why should she love me? I wasn't her fucking daughter, I was just fucking nobody, not Maria not anyone, just the bastardising devil's work. Touch me and you die.

"Wake up, wake up, a boat is missing, daughter wake up. We must go to the pier. Quickly." Standing on the wind-swept pier, frozen. Staring out at the churned-up angry waves lashing, crashing, battering all. Why the fuck did I come here? Why the fuck, bringing the evil, I have the devil's death hand. Mary is with me, her hand digging deeply into my arm, she holds me while I shake. The silence fills the wind-storm night as the lifeboat returns. The rumble goes through the crowd, one dead one alive. Anxious faces pray. I can't stop it, I can't stop it. She just holds and holds on to me.

Granddad is dead and Rory is barely alive. As we follow the ambulance to Cork I break apart, like a cheap broken glass I crash, dissolve into splinters, in the mist of her own horrendous grief she deals with mine.

The house is quiet except for the mumble of voices in the next room. I want to go run, run away take my evil with me. Why did I come here to do this? Touch me and you are dead. Granddad's waxed face lies in the good room, brown boxed still. I crouch in the corner digging the knife over and over again; watching how the skin breaks, the coldness of the blade slowly glides over it. When there is sharp pain it is good.

She finds me, my blood oozing red; she takes me in her strong arms. Gently she cleans the driven bladed skin.

"I need you now daughter, don't leave me," she whispers gently into my ear. "This is not your fault.

"He is just passing over, daughter, to the other side. You did not make this happen. Be brave. Know that you are not that powerful."

I am numb, numb to her, to the world, to all.

Rory comes home. He walks like an old man.

"Like they cut the head off me," he says, rubbing his hand on his shaved head. "Jesus" is all he can say for the next couple of weeks. "The fucking state of me. Jesus. Am I a skinhead or what." I sit forever watching him, waiting for him to die, ready to follow him, but Rory doesn't die and soon he is well enough to sit by the range. His moaning causes so much laughter that it rings through the house.

One day when we are on our own he says, "you know what. Like, I'm going back fishing. Like you'll stay with her or what," his eyes dance in his head. "Fuck she needs you

Infusions

and I need to rock," he laughs, shaking his growing red hair.

Over the months, with blessings and love, the devil dies inside of me and I begin to talk.

At eighteen I stand proud with my mother and brother and take her name.

Java Writers

Infusions

**Don't mention it
Bernadette Whyte**

Beep beep pause, beep beep pause, beep…

I'm in my swimsuit (the one with the secret make you look marvelous tummy tucking panel). The tide is coming in, the sand is golden, the wind is whirring gently and there are surfers out on the bay. In the distance I see some walkers strolling along the beach. This is amazing, amazing. No, not amazing, wait, something is not right. This is Ladies Beach. I know this place well.

   I have never seen golden sand here; I have never heard the wind whirr like this. Surely Ladies Beach is way too sheltered for surfers. No, that's not what's strange. Well, that is strange but not the strangest thing, it seems everything is in slow motion. I am floating down over the golden sand in my very expensive magic swimsuit, floating down to the slow motion moving tide that is ever so ever so ever so taking its time to come in to shore. I am floating down to the bay where the tanned surfers are surfing. Tanned? In Galway? The guys (because they are far too cool to be called men) are wearing Bermudas, not the top-to-toe wet suits of Blackrock and Galway Bay fashion. The babes (because they are far too babe-like to be called women) are surfing in slow fecking motion.

Beep beep pause, beep beep pause

Ok, ok, ok, I am awake, I'm awake. I should've known that was a dream, just a dream. Hmm, magic swimsuit howareya! I hear the windowpane as it dances along with the rain. I hear the odd car splashing through on its journey to wherever. I slowly emerge from my cosy crumpled haven. I roll over to grab the offending beep beep that has dragged me from my paradise island and think to myself why don't I just change that alarm tone to something soothing, something that will gently coax me into the day.

What! 6.15am? I must have been very, very tired when I set that alarm, I'm never up before 9am.

Beep beep pause, beep beep pause

Feck, it's a text message.

In dub, 4got name of hotel, emigration wont let us thru without address, can u go2 house, get notebook on table n txt it2me plez. sorry sis.

I'm an odd mixture of annoyed and glad, annoyed at having been woken up with a fright and glad that the news is not more serious. I scramble out of bed and while hopping out of my pyjamas I text back: *Ok will do.*

The wipers are struggling again. The rain is making fun of this little car as we plod along. Screech scratch piddle patter, screech scratch piddle patter. Somebody is saying something interesting on the radio. I hear, "and it is of the utmost importance that schwhooo... beezzzz" screech scratch piddle patter, "in this present climate". In this

Infusions

present climate I think to myself, in this present climate I will be lucky to arrive in one piece at my sister's house and get that address before they are shipped back here to this rain. That, is of the utmost importance! I turn off the radio, at least that switch works.

Beep beep pause, beep beep pause

any luck?, can you find it?

I text back: *Still in traffic*

I have a picture in my head of the *happy* family scene in Dublin airport right now. Siobhan, my sister, is probably sitting outside the emigration office; Michael, my godchild, totally pissed off because he is thirteen and in his own head too old to be going on a family holiday. Sheila, the youngest niece is no doubt driving them crazy counting every suitcase that she can see and David, my brother-in-law, is probably unsuccessfully trying to be calm and is saying things like "it's always a good idea to have one last look around in case anything is forgotten." David's mother, Maud, my sister's mother-in-law, is probably by now organising the entire airport staff to get her a nice cup of tea to help her through this trauma.

Beep beep pause, beep beep pause

Shit.

I see the one worded text pop up on the screen; I will answer it later when I am not driving. Ok, so it is worse than I thought. Siobhan rarely uses the "s" word, when she does, it means she is struggling. Maud has probably gone into the airport kitchen herself to make her own tea, as she demands a sterling silver pot and china cups.

I'm imagining scenes of hair tearing and screaming when the car in front of me suddenly comes to a stop at an amber light. Ok, maybe it is red, I don't know. I can't feckin see it through the window except in between the screech scratch swishes. I also come to a sudden stop: instinctively my eyes close as I wait for the harsh clash of metal on metal (actually in the case of my car it is more polyfiller than metal). To my shock there is no such sound.

The car is not moving, I do not hear anyone shouting at me, and I can't see anyone coming towards me either but there could be someone and I wouldn't see them with these wayward wipers.

The traffic lights are red, the blue Volvo is still in front of me. I am confused. Now in my moment of a million things going through my head all at once I think:

I must be dead, there is no way these brakes could have stopped in time to not crash into that car.

I will be dead if I don't get to that address before the flight goes.

Being dead might not be so bad really, I mean I can't imagine there is much in the way of rushing around and driving through relentless rain for one who is dead.

Dead centre, dead right, dead on, dead dead, funny oul word that really. The rain hears my thoughts and splatters big splodges of mega drops on the windscreen. It sounds like seven seagulls dancing on the tin roof of this little car. I wait for some annoyed fellow road user to appear demanding to know how I could be so stupid. I wait but there is no one rapping on the window.

No, the engine is still running, everything seems to be ok. I cannot understand it. The car must have actually stopped when I pressed on the brake, how amazing. "There is no sign of impact," I say out loud to myself. No sign of impact? I always wanted to be a highway patrol officer when I was young, I know that in Galway there wasn't much need for such a thing when I was growing up, in fact as I sit in this rain here, splitter, splatter, screech scratch piddle, patter, I am thinking there isn't much need for a highway patrol officer in Galway now. They'd be bored silly.

"Excuse me madam," the officer would say, "I see that you are stuck in traffic again," and as he or she produced a flask and a Griffins cake box, might add, "would you like a cup of tea and a muffin while you wait?"

The traffic lights go red, then green, amber, red, and green again. I decide that I must be creating my own big huge gap in the ozone layer all by myself so in a fit of guilt I stop the engine. It is peaceful now in my little yellow pod. There is no splish splash screech scratch, just the piddle patter of the rain and the sound of imaginary seagulls sean-nós dancing on the rooftop.

I practice my mindfulness. I am present to the rain and to the blurred bubbles of what must be people with umbrellas crossing this busy traffic light junction. I am aware of stray drops that sneak in through the very slight space where the windowpane does not quite reach up to the top of the window frame. I am present to how my body feels: cold, tired and wet on one side of my bum from the drops that made it into the car and onto the driver seat last night. I hear the sounds of the slow trawling cars, I smell the wet cloth of my skirt, I am present to it all and then:

Beep beep pause, beep beep pause

They r allown us 15 mins to get ur text

I am present to my panic, feckit. I text back: *Nearly there*

The lights go amber, green, and the car in front moves. I turn the key, pull out the choke, and with my feet poised over the pedals to do the necessary footwork, my hands holding the steering wheel, I lean forward out of habit, to discover I am not moving. I push in the choke, pull it out again, wait then push it in.

"Khuzzz, khuzzz," says my little yellow car.
"Feckit," says I.
"Khuzzz," says the car
"Right I better not flood you," says I.

The lights seem to speed through red, green, amber, red, green, amber. I press the hazard lights switch, nothing. I know now that it is the battery. I am present to the rain, the car not moving, the traffic lights, the scene
in Dublin airport, my wet trousers, the sweat beginning to pour from my temples, my churning stomach and then that blissful awareness that often comes at such times: "The only way is up."

There is a tapping at the window. It is a garda. I can see through the blotchy window a blurry outline of navy. Is this the highway patrol of Galway? I roll down the window, squeak, squeak it gets stuck, *shit,* squeak, squeak. There are no muffins or flask. She looks at me without saying anything but before she gets to say "ten four eleven Mary three we have a suspect here" (as they used to do with people who stopped in the middle of the highway on CHIPS) I find myself saying, "I know this is not a legal place to park and I am not parked exactly. I know that I should have the hazard lights on but they wouldn't work and I think I am having a little trouble with the battery, now it's not exactly a new battery but it is not exactly an old one either and I am aware that I may be causing a slight traffic congestion, and I know that it is early on a Monday morning and lots of people are trying to get to work and did you ever see anything like this rain and the traffic lights are going awfully fast and normally I wouldn't even be up at this hour and I know I shouldn't be blocking up the whole of Galway like this but the thing is that -"

Infusions

"Excuse me Madam," I stop talking. "I see that you are stuck in this traffic. We have a tow truck here that will assist you off the road and will take you and the car to wherever you need to be right now."

Beep beep pause, beep beep pause

10mins, so sorry bout this sis.

I am aware of the garda standing with her head bent down to look in the window as she talks to me. I ignore the text beep. In fact I find myself pretending that I do not have a phone at all, and I certainly don't have one sitting there in the passenger seat apparently having some sort of hissy fit.

The man from the tow truck has pulled up the truck beside my car. The garda car is parked in between lanes on the other side of my car. The rain has eased off and now I see that I am like a little yellow EasiSingle in a sandwich. A kind of car sandwich. I am aware that the blue lights are flashing, I hadn't noticed that until now. I took it for granted that she had rode in on a silver motorbike or something. The garda talks to the tow truck man.

Beep beep pause, beep beep... I grab the phone.

5 mins, hope ur ok

I know that if Siobhan is texting using less than 100 characters then she is under a lot of stress. I imagine that Michael has decided never to talk to his parents again, Sheila is probably going around trying to collect all the luggage trolleys and arrange them in some sort of order of cleanliness or road worthiness. David will be lying across whatever airport seats he can find, eyes closed, looking calm and pretending it's all not happening. His mother will be extolling the virtues of the organised wives of her other three boys, giving detailed examples of how utterly perfect they are, poor Siobhan.

I climb into the cab of the truck; the radio is on. "Long delays expected inbound at Newcastle, University Road and Mary's road, while Gardai are clearing an obstruction there." The truck driver changes the radio channel. I am grateful.

"Where to and are you late for work now?"

"I'm in a hurry but not to work, I have to pick up something in Lower Salthill just beside The Cottage Bar."

"Ok so."

Beep beep pause -

??

I jump out of the truck. I run to the door, I have my own key. I had my own key. Where the feck is it? I always have it in the ashtray in the car. Oh no. I run back to the tow truck, I ignore the startled look of the tow truck driver as I hoist myself up onto the back of the truck. I struggle to hoist my long gypsy style skirt up onto the back of the truck with me. The car is not locked. I do not notice that I am doing a tightrope style walk along the side of the car (I remember this later in flashbacks of the event). I open the door, lean in to the ashtray, catch the bottom of my skirt on some sort of clamp that is attached to the bottom of the car to keep it in place, I grab the key:

Beep beep pause, beep beep….

I ignore this as I try to get my battered self down off the truck with some sense of decorum. Once on terra firma I smooth down what is left of my skirt and run to the front door.

Infusions

Beep beep pause, beep beep…

I open it, run to the table, I press reply and with practiced fingers text the address to the waiting tableaux in the airport.

    I find myself strolling back out to the tow truck. The truck driver is drinking from a bottle of water. I tell myself that he must be used to seeing strange actions in his line of work.

    "Everything ok?"

    I nod.

    "Where do you want the car? I can leave it at a garage for you if you want?"

    I give my mechanic's name and address.

    The tow truck pulls off with my little yellow car on it. The door is slightly open, the window is rattling, there are no seagulls on the rooftop. I go to a nearby café. I am imagining that cup of tea and the muffin.

    I sit down.

Beep beep pause, beep beep pause

We r thru, thanx a million sis, hope twasnt 2much truble

I text back: *DMI*

Java Writers

Infusions

An Indian Summer
Lorna Moynihan

"June 21st, longest day of the year, and that was *Mr Blue Sky* from ELO to cheer us all up on this wet summer morning," the chirpy radio announcer says just before the radio pips the early morning news.

As Maura stretches in the bed, her thoughts focus on the day ahead. "June 21st, longest day of the year," she says to herself, the start of summertime. As she pulls herself up and sits on the edge of the bed, she pauses; a year ago she would have contemplated getting back under the covers and staying in bed all day. Not now: she's up and as she pulls the blinds to look out at the now familiar landscape of rugged Connemara, Maura sighs. "Weather forecasters got it right," she says to herself as she looks at the misty rain coming in from the Atlantic, the rain forming a heavy veil over the Aran Islands as they disappear in the distance. Maura looks out at the lushness of her own garden, as the rain gives her flowers and vegetables a gentle watering. Maura smiles to herself in a content sort of way.

"Is this happiness?" she asks herself. Yes, she is happy, happy with her small bungalow in Connemara, happy with her garden, happy as she can be, but there will always be something, someone missing from this picture.

Maura first arrived in Connemara in the early 1960s as a newlywed with her husband Peadar. They had travelled over on honeymoon to visit their extended families in Galway and Kerry. They had a small wedding in England, with the reception in the local Irish club in Manchester. It had been a whirlwind romance, and to be fair they hadn't given either set of parents much notice of their wedding. Maura had only been in England for six months when she met Peadar. She had left a small village near the town of Dingle in Kerry to join her sister Anne in England; she had hoped to train as a children's nurse, and had just started her training in the Royal Manchester Children's Hospital when she met Peadar at a dance in an Irish club.

    She pretended not to see him at first when he gave her a cheeky wink as he danced around the hall with another girl on his arm. What she did notice was that he was tall, very good looking with dark wavy hair. When he asked her to dance, Maura felt all the other girls' eyes watching their every move on the dance floor. He was a great dancer; as they swayed and jived to the music he held her tight, so tight that she had difficulty breathing. She was shy at first, and didn't want to appear too forward. When she finally dared to look up, she noticed that his eyes were green, sparkling and full of laughter. His face was tanned from working outside, and his hands, while rough with calluses from the physical work, still held her gently.

    As they danced he told her all about himself, that he was the middle son of a family of five from Connemara in the West of Ireland. He told her he had left home to make his fortune in England, knowing that the small family farm could only ever support his eldest brother. They laughed as they danced, as he told her of his new life in England. He told her he worked hard six days a week, building the new

Infusions

suburbs of Greater Manchester, and that he shared a room in digs with three other men. Maura told him of her plans to become a children's nurse and how many of her family were in England.

Peadar and Maura soon became a couple. They met every Saturday night at the dances in the Irish clubs that were scattered all around Manchester. Many of Ireland's top show bands like *The Royal Show Band* travelled to England to play for the young Irish now working and living in England. Maura and Peadar always went to the pictures on a Sunday afternoon in the Odeon Cinema. They alternated between a Western or war film one week and a romance or musical the next. They held hands in the dark and Peadar would try and get a kiss. Maura wasn't prudish but she had respect for herself and Peadar had to be reminded a few times about roaming hands. He teased her soft Kerry accent with his thick West of Ireland brogue, which was speckled with Gaelic words from his childhood of speaking Irish at home. He liked to call her *a Stòr*, my darling, he wasn't afraid to show his emotions, he was different from the other men she had met before and Maura liked that about him.

It didn't take Maura long to fall in love with this man from Connemara, who had big plans for his future. He told her he would learn a trade and then have his own business some day. Maura was even more delighted when he told her that she too was a big part of his plans for the future. Maura never did finish her nursing training, Peadar was adamant that he would provide for his family, and he didn't want his wife to work. It was a norm then for a wife to stay at home, it was something that Maura did regret in later life. They married, initially rented a small flat, Maura was pregnant within the first year and happily settled to become a homemaker. As three more children arrived in quick succession, they eventually bough a small house in the suburbs.

Java Writers

Every summer they travelled back to Ireland for their holidays, they would drive and take the ferry from Holyhead to Dublin, their four children asleep in the back. The children would say later how they loved their holidays when they would go to sleep in England and wake up in Ireland. They were happy days. In the early years they travelled to Kerry first and then onto Connemara, but as the years went by Maura's parents died, and while her elder brother, who inherited the farm, extended an open invitation, Maura knew that her sister-in-law was not so willing to entertain them.

While Maura missed Kerry, she also grew to love Connemara. She loved the freedom her children had, their laughter carrying on the air as they played with their many cousins on the haystacks in the small fields near their grandparents' house, or down at the beach as they dared and raced each other into the cold sea. Maura especially loved the long evenings in the West of Ireland, with the light in the sky till 11 o'clock at night, the wide setting sun filling the sky with a hue of colours from deep reds to dusty pink. As they walked along the lane edged with fuchsia to the beach, the sun always seemed to linger on the sea for the longest time as if reluctant to leave their peaceful corner of the world behind for another day. The bracing salty wind that drove the waves in from the Atlantic during the day also seemed to have less vigour in the evenings, as if it too had spent its energy for that day.

Mostly though, she loved the time she spent with Peadar. It was a time to catch up with each other, a time to talk, to make plans and discuss the future. It was like they were on their honeymoon all over again, as they would take a walk each evening.

As they sat and watched the sun setting into the western sky during those holidays, they talked about their plans for the future. Maura could always tell when Peadar was working through a plan. His brain went into overdrive; he would be excited and animated at first, hardly containing his enthusiasm. These plans, like all great plans, often started out on the back of a cigarette pack, and then later Maura would find scraps of paper in his pockets when washing, or stuffed down the sides of the couch.

Peadar worked hard and eventually it paid off. He had started his own building company as he had said he would and it had become very successful. His plan was to retire comfortably and pass on the business to his son Peter who had joined in the business after studying engineering in university. Their other children, "all university educated" as Peadar took delight in telling his old building friends from his digs, were all married and settled with their own families.

By now too, Maura had begun to feel somewhat redundant, her days occupied with the odd grandchild babysitting duty or helping out with some parish or other fund raising event. When Peadar retired (and golf was never going to be on the agenda for him) they travelled, short city breaks in Europe, occasional sun holidays in Spain, one time taking the grandchildren to Disneyland in America, but they both agreed, nothing could match their family holidays in Connemara, and that's when they decided to retire back in Ireland. They bought a small bungalow near Carraroe in Connemara. They moved in early March, hoping to have the house ready for their children and grandchildren visiting in August. They enjoyed setting up another home together, picking out paint colours for the walls, visiting furniture showrooms and garden centres. However, getting the new home ready was tiring; Maura remarked that they were "not young honeymooners now!" as they fell into bed exhausted from their long work filled days. They still made time for their walks in the evenings, still made plans for this and that, more travel and the garden, they discussed maybe getting a glasshouse "to grow some tomatoes" Peadar said.

Java Writers

    Maura noticed that Peadar was starting to have forty winks in the chair after dinner. It wasn't like him but sure wasn't that what retirement was all about? That's where she found him, as if sleeping, the doctors said that the toll of a life of physical work had eventually caught up with him and he had had a massive heart attack. She was glad when the doctor said that he hadn't suffered. Peadar had hardly ever been sick in his life and Maura knew that he would have wanted to go fast, no sickness, no fuss. They were barely four months into their retirement.

That first summer passed by Maura as if in a haze. Of course, the children and grandchildren all came. Peadar, according to his wishes, was cremated, and his ashes scattered into Galway Bay, on the very beach where they had made their plans on all those summer holidays. Maura was left a widow in what was now to her a strange country. Although born in Ireland, and considering herself Irish, having lived in Manchester for the best part of forty years Maura often had to remind herself that she lived here now and was not just on holidays. She had of course contemplated going back to Manchester, but they had sold their home, and the economic downturn had affected her financial standing. Her children tried to coax her to return, but she didn't feel like being a burden to them. They had their own families now and their own lives.
    When that first winter came, Maura gratefully took refuge in the shorter days, the fire in the range on throughout the day. She felt justified in pulling her curtains at 4 o'clock in the day, locking out the world. She would sit in her favourite armchair, a throw casually laid across her legs, the television listings page open, ticking off the programmes she would watch that evening. She had a routine; she preferred it that way. She would watch *The Afternoon Programme*; she loved the health and fashion sections, her namesake Maura Derrane with her soothing

voice and lovely personality as familiar to Maura as an old friend. Later she'd watch Daithí O'Shea: he was another favourite, his Kerry lilt reminding her of her own father's voice, a distant memory from her own childhood. She'd make her tea while the 6 o'clock news was on, only half listening, she wouldn't pretend or care to understand the talk of bank bailouts and foreign countries going bankrupt. The latest unemployment figures didn't mean much to her either, and any news story about crime in rural Ireland only made Maura more aware of her own isolation.

As winter slowly eased into the spring, many of these now familiar programmes took their annual break. Maura missed their familiar voices coming into her sitting room. As far as television went, Maura didn't venture too far from the home channels of RTE 1 & 2, her childhood Irish now long forgotten, unable to help her understand the presenters on the Irish channel TG4. The newer channel of TV3 just seemed to be filled with American crime or teenage dramas. She did miss the BBC channels, especially the Sunday afternoon old films and the costume dramas. Thankfully, the soaps like *Coronation Street* gave her some continuity. It was often painful listening to the Manchester accents, reminding her of another life, a life she had now left behind.

There was no catalyst, no eureka moment. Maura just knew she couldn't go on like this indefinitely. "No one can help you except yourself" her sister Anne said on the phone from Manchester. Was she too old to make a new start, make new friends? She never really had a problem making friends; her friends in the past were closely associated with where her life was at that time. Her friends were the other mothers she met at the school gates, friends she met at the local fundraiser coffee mornings, friends through the Irish club. Friends she seemed to have for a lifetime, friends now living in another country. If Maura was to make a new start, she had to have closure.

She spent a week replying to the mass cards and condolence letters she had received after Peadar's death. She knew people meant well and she felt guilty, having neglected replying sooner. In the pile she was surprised to find an official letter that had somehow been unopened. It was the envelope that contained their Irish bus passes. Peadar had joked the day he posted off the forms, saying "there will be no stopping us now, we can travel and see the whole country, we might even go to Dublin just for our lunch."

That's exactly what Maura did. She knew she was running away. Away from the quietness of the house, the idle chatter in the local shop about the inclement Irish weather, away from the kind neighbours who kept inviting her around for a chat and a glass of wine. She knew they meant well, but she wasn't ready for that just yet.

She'd get on the bus in the morning, not sure where she would end up: Limerick or Sligo, sometimes going as far as Dublin just for lunch. As the months went by, she'd often just stay in Galway, she would spend the day walking the small narrow streets. It was a city as compact as a village. She loved the sound of the seagulls as she walked down High Street reminding her that the sea was not far away.

Its busy streets were full of tourists eagerly listening to their guide as they stood outside Lynch's Castle. Maura would watch the street entertainers and buskers, who seemed to be on every corner regardless of the weather, their antics bringing laughter to the crowd. This laughter was infectious and Maura began to heal. She had a routine: she would visit Easons or Charlie Byrne's bookshop where she'd buy the latest Booker prize winner or reacquaint herself with old favourites such as Maeve Binchy or Edna O'Brien. She'd have lunch in McCambridge's, browse the clothes racks in Anthony Ryans. In Griffins Bakery she'd indulge in a Princes Finger and a milky coffee as a treat before getting the bus back home.

Infusions

Over the next few months, Maura got to know and greet Tom the bus driver on a first name basis. She'd smile and say hello to the other passengers on the bus into Galway: The two Misses Burkes, retired spinster sisters, travelling into Galway to go to mass in the Abbey church every day and then have their lunch in the GBC restaurant; Noel, a retired guard, studying a course in history at the university. "My wife encourages me to go," he'd laugh, "says I am only in her way around the house." Finally there was Pat, a widower, like Maura, trying to readjust to life on his own, who would smile and give her that reassuring nod that told her that he too knew what she was going through. As time passed Maura would often sit with the Burke sisters telling them about the newest play she had seen at the Town Hall theatre, or tell Noel about a fascinating talk she'd attended at the city library. She talked about books with Pat, an avid reader like her; they'd discuss the latest books they had read. She told him about a notice in the library to join a book club.

"Maybe you could start one here in the autumn in the local community centre," he said to her.

Maura is brought back to the present as she hears the post land on the mat in the hall. "More junk mail," she thinks to herself.

After her breakfast, Maura's morning flies by. She is happy, happier than she has been for quite some time. As the rain stops she heads into her garden; she talks over the wall to some French tourists who are looking for the coral strand.

She spends the next few hours deadheading flowers, sowing cucumber seeds and replanting up some lettuce. She writes a note to remind herself to give some tomatoes to Noel and his wife Mary, as a thank you for inviting her to dinner the previous Saturday.

Java Writers

It's almost 12 o'clock; Maura puts the kettle on for a cup of tea with her lunch. Pat phones for a chat and to check what time he is coming over to discuss the book club.

After lunch, as Maura sits in her garden finishing off her cup of tea with a biscuit, she waves to her neighbours, Michael and Kitty. In the background, people on the radio complain to Joe Duffy about being overcharged for tea and scones on the Ring of Kerry. As the rain starts to fall again, Maura retreats further under the parasol.

"There is always the hope of an Indian summer!" Michael her neighbour says cheerily over the fence.

"Yes there is," Maura laughs in reply.

Infusions

Infusions

Swimming with the sprat
Ann Flynn

It's almost nine
and sunlight tilts
the evening sky
across the water.
I walk a ragged line
to the shore.

The wind interrogates
my skin and I answer
to a waist's depth.
And then I see them there,
a thousand tiny fish
hiding in the tide.

Further out,
a frenzy of sea gulls
plunge through a purple sky.
I pray that the water is empty.

Tomorrow I'll be at my desk,
holding myself intact,
and when the gulls are crowding me,
I'll be swimming with the sprat.

Java Writers

On this bright day

On this bright day,
the wind torments my scarf
until it loses all composure and unravels.

And the lifeguard's flag,
longing to be carried away,
protests against the pole with every blast.

And even as the waves pull out from the shore
they cling to the shingle and
come rushing back.

The thought of you
reaches through the length of me
until my limbs ache as if they were growing again.

And with the waves and the wind
and the vanquished flag
I wait for you.

Fire Dance
Nataraja destroys the world from our hearts.

Even in this hopeless silence, He is dancing,
burning through our hours,
until we are nameless in the empty spaces
of other people's lives,
and still He turns, opening His hand to the devouring star.

I hold your hand in the quivering air,
close my eyes and try to picture not being here,
like the sun imagining the night sky.
But somehow I am always the observer.

And you watch me from the place
that you have watched the moving world,
never quite still enough to find its centre,
you always turn away, but He is dancing.
And when at last He takes your hand,
I'll torch my heart and burn with you.

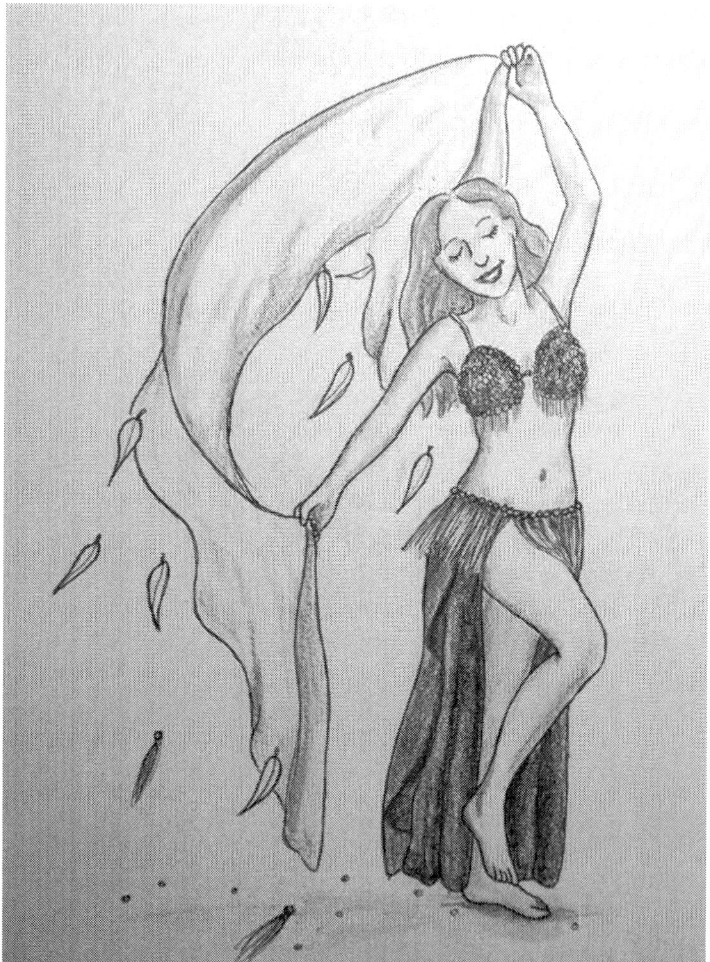

Dance into Danger
Yvonne McEvaddy

I'll never forget that night.

It was the night of the competition I'd been preparing for the past few months. I had just spent some glorious moments gliding across the stage, with the greens and blues of my costume shimmering in the lights, all of life's worries evaporating as I danced to one of my favourite Egyptian tunes, my arms flowing with the rhythm of the flute, my belly gyrating to the beat of the drum. It's a freedom I only ever felt when either dancing or meditating, both daily rituals for me. Each day always brought with it at least two blissful hours that were all my own.

Up to that point there had been no obstacle in my life that I hadn't been able to overcome using these methods of coping. It was very often in the moments of clarity after I finished my morning meditations that the solutions came to me. Therefore I generally came across as a free-spirited, well-balanced person, which is why I had such a large clientele coming to me to solve their problems using aromatherapy and crystals. People trusted in my abilities to solve their problems, as they could see that I had my own life well in hand.

Therefore, it came as a complete shock to find myself, having shimmied gracefully off-stage, stumbling into the arms of a man. This was my time to be full of poise, and so my first reaction, apart from shock, was one of annoyance that this person had invaded my space. However, I barely had time to register these emotions as, before I knew it, the man had spun me around and, with one hand over my mouth, his other hand gripped me tightly. Fear had me very firmly in its grasp.

Taking a deep breath, I tried to focus my mind, but it was impossible. I tried to remember my self defence, but found myself stumped. Realising that I was being dragged towards the back exit, I became even more panicked.

The trunk of a car was opened. I was released with a thud. Just before the lid was slammed shut, enveloping me in darkness, I caught a glimpse of the man who had taken me. It was Jack, my friend Anne's husband. I wondered if Anne was behind this. My birthday was the next day. Maybe I was being kidnapped and brought to my birthday party. He must have gotten it wrong. Surely he was to have waited for the finish of Anne's performance, even if it wasn't practical to wait to see who had won the competition.

I hammered on the lid of the trunk, and called out, "Jack, the joke's over. I know it's you. Come on, let me out. I'll still pretend I'm shocked and surprised when I get there."

There was no response. I heard the engine turning over. I wondered what the purpose was in trying to frighten the life out of me before springing a surprise party on me. Maybe it was because I was so fond of mob movies that they thought it would be fun if I spent a few minutes wondering how I was to be killed. It would be just like Anne to come up with something like that. I started giggling as I thought of all the movies I had watched where a person was put in the trunk of a car before a lump of concrete was tied to their feet and they were thrown in to sleep with the fish, or were buried alive, or were brought into a room covered in plastic and had a bullet put in their head.

The car went over a large bump, knocking me around in the trunk. I stopped laughing, and started to panic instead. The joke had gone too far. I took several deep breaths. The stuffy space and the smell of car fumes did nothing to aid me into a calm frame of mind. If anything, the more deep breaths I took the more I struggled to breathe, as the confines of the trunk closed in on me.

The car came to a stop. Although daylight was fading I was dazzled by the sudden brightness that assailed my eyes as the lid opened. Once again I felt Jack's grip around my waist as he lifted me out. He threw me over his shoulder and, wondering if I was wrong, if maybe it wasn't my friend's husband after all, I started to scream, kick my legs and flail my arms at my assailant, who continued carrying me deep into the woods.

My arm caught briefly on a branch, before I heard a rip. *This couldn't be Jack*, I realised. *He would have more respect for my costume. Anne owns enough of them that he knows how much they cost.* I kicked and screamed more furiously now, sending buttons and tassels flying from my torn costume.

When we came to a stop I was thrown to the ground. My head banged off something hard and I put my hand up to rub the lump that was forming. Through my blurred vision I saw the telltale tattoo of an eagle on the man's arm. The sneer on his broad face was an unfamiliar expression, though.

When I came to, it was to find myself sitting beside Jack in the passenger seat of his car. We went over a bump in the road and my already sore head banged off the window. I didn't know him that well and, seeing the maniacal look on his face, started to wonder if I knew him at all. The one thing I thought I knew about him had turned out to be a lie.

Anne had rung me one night to ask if I could help, as Jack was having trouble in the bedroom department. She had seemed embarrassed to be asking, said that I must never mention it because it would make him feel like less of a man. I had promised that I would never say anything about it to anyone, and had suggested he drink an infusion of nettle leaf and ginseng tea, and also that Anne give him a full-body massage using sandalwood, coriander and lime oils. Although he was a large man and didn't seem to be in short supply of testosterone, in my professional capacity I had seen men bigger than him with similar problems.

It was only weeks later when I asked Anne how things were going and she had replied that everything was great with Vincent that I realised she was having an affair, that it wasn't Jack who was suffering from erectile dysfunction, but her new lover.

Anne had confided that there had been no intimacy between herself and her husband for a long time, and when she'd met sensitive and poetic Vincent, the attraction had been instant, his home in the mountains making the perfect lovers' retreat. Even when Vincent started having trouble she stood by him, helped him through it because she loved him more than she'd ever loved her husband, and feared that Jack had overheard her on the phone the day she asked for help with his libido.

I tried to talk to Jack, asked him to tell me what was wrong, but he said nothing. I filled the silence with my own thoughts. I wanted to be at home with my husband, Mike. I thought of him picking up a bottle of the latest elixir I had made, juniper berry and sandalwood, him opening the bottle and taking a whiff, before scrunching up his nose and putting the cap back on the bottle. He loved to call me his white witch, loved to watch me mixing oils, but sometimes found the scents a bit overpowering. I wondered what was

Infusions

to become of me; was Jack just trying to teach me to keep my nose out of other people's business, or did he have something more sinister in mind? Would I ever see Mike's smile and feel his tender touch again?

After some time, Jack banged his fist on the steering wheel, causing me to jump. He started to mutter. I strained my ears to hear.

Then he yelled, "Damn you to hell, Anne, and you too, Sally for making that fucker's dick work again."

I cowered in my seat, knowing that Anne's suspicions were correct. Seeing the road winding upwards ahead, I suspected we were heading in the direction of Vincent's house.

Earlier I had wondered how long I had lost consciousness for, but with the sun rising over the mountains, casting a pink glow on the lush green hills I knew it had been for a quite a while. I hoped for Anne's sake that we wouldn't pull up to see a silhouette of her and Vincent making love, as Jack already looked like he was ready to spill some blood.

Jack pulled up outside the house, and got out of the car. He opened the back door of the car and grabbed an axe from behind my seat. I jumped out and said, "Jack, wait, what are you thinking?" Then realisation struck; I should be wondering what I was thinking coming between a man with an axe and his intended purpose.

I stood back and watched as he forced his way through the door. The banging woke Vincent and when Jack entered the house, with me following at a short distance, he was faced with a very sleepy and stunned man. He ran at Vincent, swinging the axe. I looked on in disbelief as blood splattered across the room. He didn't stop until the other man was no longer recognisable, organs spilling out of a body that was slashed first in half, then in quarters. He left the axe embedded in Vincent's head, the eyeballs hanging out like a gross caricature.

He used the bathroom to clean up afterwards while I went outside and retched. I didn't throw up, although so nauseous I couldn't stand up, just slumped against the car, taking big gulps of air.

To see Jack coming out of the house, you wouldn't think he had just hacked a man to pieces. Not even giving me a glance, he tossed the axe into the car and hopped in. He cursed as he turned the key in the engine and it didn't start. I moved away from the car, having no desire to get back in with him, knowing now what he was capable of. However, sometime between him getting out to look under the bonnet and him taking off, I saw myself drift into the passenger seat, without any recollection of opening the door.

He floored the accelerator, picking up so much speed that everything outside the window was just a blur. He started muttering again, a smile on his face as he said, "Now, Anne, it's your turn."

The sound of the sirens had me looking behind us and when I looked to the front again I saw a sign for loose chippings, but Jack mustn't have seen it until it was too late. As the car was flipping over my life didn't flash before my eyes, instead it was memories of my death...

I came to in the forest and saw Jack holding a knife over me. I screamed, the knife slicing through my stomach. Then I watched as he washed his hands and the knife in the stream. The next time I came to I was in the passenger seat of his car, the memories of my death washed clear from my mind in the bloodied waters of the stream.

As the car came to a stop, righting itself, the door was yanked open. Jack was dragged out and placed under arrest.

He now has a high price to pay for the murders, for his wife's affair: a lifetime in prison. I, on the other hand, am spending eternity in my favourite costume, listening to my favourite Egyptian tune, the greens and blues shimmering as I dance around Mike. He seems to be consoled, to sense my presence, when the silky costume brushes against his skin.

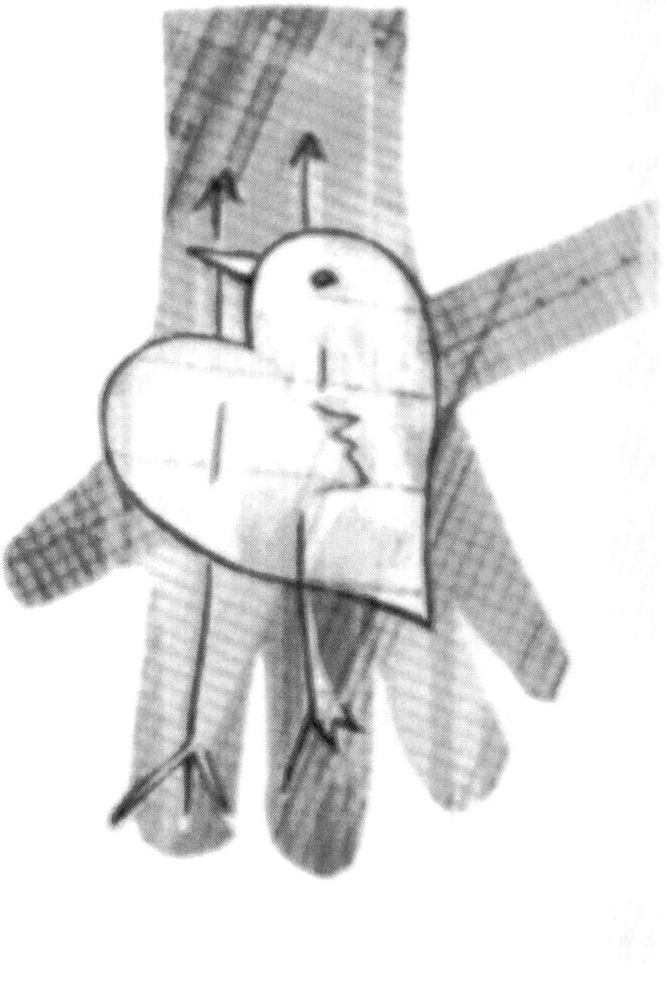

Infusions

God's Gift
Evelyn Parsons

Breasts are his specialty. His area of expertise. They keep him busy, these frontloaded patients, tremulous, even now in the height of Summer. Unruly hope and dread escaping their brassieres. It's not as if he's the only breast man around, but they say he's the best, and that's saying something- for his is a Centre of Excellence.

For two years now, our diaries, his Excellency's and mine, have been synchronized. A routine scheduled for our routine. Monthly appointments dates I mark in red: April, May, June. January was skipped entirely because of a paper he delivered in the Royal College; February, because of a conference in Chicago. March was my fault. Well, not fault exactly. Fault is the wrong word and we're discovering just how much the correct word matters. Reason is better. I am the reason for missing March. I was in hospital myself then, two floors below him, having more tests.

That's when we agreed no matter what, before my results even came back, we wouldn't use that word.

"Sometimes, these things just happen," he said. "This is nobody's fault."

And because it's still nobody's fault we're back at it again. He fits me in on red ringed days, - or rather, I fit him in. Either way it's late when he gets round to me, and he's yawning, loosening his tie and smelling of hospital. By then, he's jaded by constant female demands, already spent by endless examinations, by swishing and un-swishing curtains, behind which, hopeful double and single breasted women eye him, and sometimes women with no breasts at all, just angry red scars on their chests like worried slanted eyebrows.

So this morning, and only because I complained, he feels mine first. His brief perfunctory prelude to the main event. His busman's holiday, I think, - and not for the first time - all work and no foreplay. No after-play either. We're getting on with it and that's the important thing. He's rough, clinical, pressurized, and straight to it. I'm still partially dressed like the king-sized bed when he finishes, withdraws, and flops onto his pillow. And when the radio alarm goes off, it's as if we've won. Somehow we've beaten the clock, stolen something from the day - ahead already before the traffic updates start.

"I wish I could spare more time, darling," he says, though time has become more my problem. He kisses me quickly, swings out of bed and pads towards the shower.

"It's quality not quantity that matters," I say to his retreating naked back, "and your contribution is nonetheless greatly appreciated."

It's out before I can stop myself, sounding prissy and clipped instead of the lighter tone I strive for these days. Sometimes, just sometimes, I wish I could just shut the fuck up. Words just spill out of this mouth of mine surprising me with their tactlessness as much as anyone. I can't tell if he's heard above the radio and splashing water because he doesn't show feelings - the medical training probably- but he must feel all the same. He simply powers ahead, restraining worry behind pinstripes like prison bars.

Infusions

Morning sunlight falls on him as he towels dry and gets dressed. He's a very handsome man with or without clothes. I like watching him. Within reach and mine before he's taken captive by all those women.

"You scrub up well," I say.

He smiles though it's an old joke now, and dangles some ties towards me.

I shuffle up the bed for a better look, lean forward. I like being the one giving advice, being an expert on something.

"The burnt sienna one with flecks of umber. Matches your eyes."

He puts the others away. And I like that. With the precision of a surgical knot, he deftly loops it over and under, pulls, jiggles, pushes and the noose tightens. He moves towards the door, arms first, wrists extended, fiddling with buttonholes. His cufflinks are handcuffs, and he's being led away with no resistance.

But it's nobody's fault Officer.

Completing this month's chart, I return it and the thermometer to the bedside locker. July, my birthday month, gets ticked done. Another year cycles pointlessly by, taking with it another ten per cent. I slam the drawer on it, then get up and follow his scent to the kitchen.

Aftershave mingles in the morning air with the aroma of singed toast, blending, making a third smell, - a burnt musky tang. All male. Cup in hand, he's circling the granite island, mobile phone to ear, eyebrow cocked, pacing. His brown gaze sharpens as he listens, answers, decides, directs. The coffee machine, his favourite gadget, obliges at his press of a button, its speed of delivery titrated to the measure of his patience, its flavour to his preference. Sounds leak from his phone.

"Admissions, beds… discharges … wards … clinics…."

I scramble eggs on the hob. Rashers sizzle.

He doesn't know what time he'll be home, he says between mouthfuls. Late, anyway. His list is long today - biopsies, mastectomies, lumpectomies. Heaving clinics await, packed with women who really need to see him.

I don't complain. I've nothing to complain about. I'm grateful he could fit me in at all, considering the waiting list of the Befores - the women desperate for his touch. Women who can't wait to join the Afters - the really lucky ones. Those ones who come up to him, at charity events, during dinner parties, in restaurants, thanking God, thanking him. Or if they can't thank him, thanking me. *Me*. As if his gift had somehow rubbed off on me or I had in some unknowable way bestowed it on him for their benefit.

"What are you doing today?" he says, slicking his damp hair backwards with a comb.

Today however, I don't feel like inventing exciting accounts of planned mopping and marinating while I mope about waiting. This has been dragging on for some time.

"They should have been read by now," I say, ignoring his question.

He flicks on the giant plasma screen instead of meeting my eyes. The morning is hot and the forecaster says it's going to get hotter. I don't know why he wants the weather, what difference will it make - he's in a climate controlled environment all day, everyday.

"Surely they are read by now," I say. "It's been weeks."

He flicks off the TV.

"But don't you think… Why are they taking so blooming long?" I say. "If there was anything wouldn't…" I stop, hearing doubt and worry infecting my voice, my own grating petulance.

His eyes study at his watch again, avoiding mine. "I'll ring you."

"For sure?"

"For sure."

Infusions

"But when? I'm afraid it will be too late. This is going on -"

"Today," he says, cutting me off. "They'll be back today. For sure." His tone tells me to drop it.

I put my arms around him then, lean my head on his chest, hugging his solidness like I'm squeezing hope itself. "They'll be normal," I whisper to his soap scented neck. "I'm sure they'll be. I just need to know. *We* both need to know. Either way." I stand back, breathe deeply and try to smile. "You understand that don't you?"

He stares through the kitchen window, to beyond the clipped box hedge, to the curved drive where his jeep is parked like a getaway car, already pointing workwards.

I hand him a food container. A balanced lunch - a product of a new nutritional approach I'm following lately. He doesn't take it right away, keeps me waiting in my nightdress, arm outstretched, my offering ignored until I joke about cutting out the middle man and taking the food straight to the bin.

"Try and make sure you eat something right." I pat his arm, peck him goodbye, and say, "and... ring me."

I don't know what more I can do. There is nothing for it but to wait and that, at least, is something I'm good at.

"He can't take a call right now." The receptionist is cranky when I call back again. "If it's urgent, you can talk to one of his team or else you can make an appointment. Let's see... He can fit you in Wednesday the 12th. How about two o'clock?"

"No. That won't be necessary," I mumble, embarrassed the receptionist might deck it's me and annoyed when she doesn't.

"No news is good news," he answers himself when I ring his office at lunchtime.

"No news is no news," I say, but he has already put the phone down.

It's the dead centre of summer, - it's hot, stifling. The weather forecaster got it right for once. Purple and white lobelia trail from hanging baskets in wilting wisps. The hose spurts, snaking rivulets on the patio, and staining the earth dark around the roses. Thirsty foliage catches as much water as it can before reluctantly stalling its loss. In a slithering sliding ballet, drops linger, coalesce and fall, then leaves lift as though recoiling in grief.

Inside, the house is quiet apart from sounds of traffic passing and muffled shouts of children at play filtering through open windows. I open the post, check emails. There are greetings from friends in Australia, photo attachments: barbeques, smoking, drinking, children splashing in pools.

My, how they have grown... I reply.

There are the usual online alerts and offers in my inbox - last minute flights, family deals, Viagra spammers and ... oh God...the Agency's reply. Trembling, I oscillate between guilt, excitement and disloyalty. My finger hovers, hesitates, and hovers again. It's too soon to open it, too soon to delete it. Besides, I...*we*... still don't know. I shut down the computer instead.

This day should be like any other - eating the right things, doing the right things, thinking the right things. My life ticking by. Folic acid at nine. Tick. Calcium rich snack at eleven. Tick.

Gym at four sounds like a proper date - not the ones I'm sick of, the red ringed ones. My session today is thirty minutes of resistance training. When I started the healthy stuff I could barely lift a double cappuccino, but commitment to regular exercise, forcing myself even on tired days, has made me stronger, healthier, and fitter surely.

Infusions

Fit for nothing it seems.

So today instead, I decide I'll spend thirty minutes resisting training. Won't that count?

Listless, I wander the house looking to return displaced things to their rightful spots. Nothing has changed since yesterday, or the day before, or the day before that.

In the pastel papered bedroom next to ours, I open the window wide. Everything in this room is wooden and distressed, and in it, I coordinate perfectly. Impulsively, I toss the coverlet. Standing back, I admire my crinkled work like the artist I used to be before creativity deserted. Squinting slightly, head to one side, I evaluate the composition. That's better, I decide, but it needs something more. Something to soften the edges. Pillows? They cascade as I throw them on the floor. I yank the curtains from their perfect symmetry, in their sentry positions, guarding light in and light out. Not quite there yet. Tugging lockers, opening wardrobes, I look for something, anything, to fling.

Everything's empty.

On the chest of drawers, under a fringed lamp, rests a Mickey Mouse bowl we picked up years ago on honeymoon in Orlando, filled now with fading potpourri. I grab and scatter handfuls in the air. They fall like red drops against the carpet, a stark haemorrhage of rose petals enlivening its neutrality. I up-end the entire bowl of dried up blooms. A painful pleasantness fills me as preserved petals spill ferric red on the soft beige pile like a letting of blood. I feel a give within, a release, something minimally destructive, leaving no visible scars. A self-mutilation by proxy. For the first time I vaguely understand cutters, those teenage girls, mostly, that I read about in problem pages while scanning for my own.

I stick to texting and checking phone messages in between cleaning bathrooms one and four. At bathroom five, I leave a shrill message on his message minder.

"I'm not worried about your waiting list. I'm worried about you, me. Us. We're waiting too long."

An hour drags. Nothing. My worry ripens to anger.

"You should call me, tell me..." I snap into the handset, "*properly* tell me. Not just fob me off between clinics and ward rounds. The results. I mean... I still don't know."

I root out the steam cleaner from the useless presents box. Steam hisses and spits in difficult to reach places. It happens after all, there is a perfect time to try it. Ringing back that bitch of a receptionist too, and asking for an appointment with my husband is beginning to sound reasonable.

Goddamit I've waited long enough. I'll give it another half an hour and if I don't hear from him by then, I'll ring back that snotty bitch and ask... no... not ask, demand, to be put straight through.

Straight through, that's right. No excuses, I'll say. *Immediately... Yes, immediately.* As haughty as I can. *Who am I? Indeed! Of course this instant, this very instant, under no circumstances can I wait, unless he's-*

Oh. Unless he... I hadn't thought of... What if he's not there... He should be there. There or in outpatients or on a ward round or in theatre. Oh... theatre. Not if he is in theatre. I won't bother him if he's in theatre. How could I? I can't expect him to leave some poor unconscious girl, breast sliced open, lobules bulging out, to come to the phone to talk to *me*. Me of the two redundant breasts. He's too professional, too full of integrity and mindful of his ethical responsibilities to do that anyway.

That's why I love him.

Infusions

Why I hate him.

I'm trying to imagine him, playing God in theatre but the Green Giant jingle from the TV commercial plays on a loop in my head. Masked, capped, gowned and green, coming to the phone with bloody gloves? He'd never.

Ah! He would get a theatre nurse of course, to hold the phone to his ear, away a bit so as not to contaminate the sterile field. Or maybe they would use speakers and my voice would be boomed around the theatre. Yes, that's what they would do.

The nurse would nod to her colleague to leave off using the suction machine. The slurping noise would cease and they would temporarily silence too the sizzle of the diathermy probe to allow clear communication of the urgent message. Mozart, his all time favourite composer, would be lowered, maybe even switched off. There would be the clink and clatter of a discarded forceps. They would all be listening, the team, hanging onto their retractors, wondering what could be so important, so urgent, so absolutely blooming crucial, that it couldn't wait until a life was saved. It would have to be crucial, wouldn't it, a matter of life or death, otherwise it would wait until the patient was safely off the table, snatched from agonies of death or disease by the steel instruments and steely nerve of this omnipotent surgeon.

The entire team, vigilant to the wound's weeping, would watch and dab and listen, while the soft calming puff of the self-inflating respiratory machine took deep steadying breaths for them all.

For me too. I would be put on loudspeaker for sure. I wouldn't dare ask then, that's what he'd think. He'd blink towards the body-less speaker; his magnifying glasses perched on his nose, rims resting on the paper mask.

"Yes?" he'd bark, waiting, his eyes would flick upwards, over his gold rims to the clock, to the Anaesthetist, to the dials, to the tubing and drains before continuing his snipping and tying and stemming of bloody flows.

"Yes? What is it? An emergency?"

I'd clam up then. Be unable to say that which couldn't *under any circumstances* wait.

"Yes?" he'd say irritated, louder this time.

The machines would be bleeping in the background, quietly at first, then insistently, signalling blood pressure dropping or pulse rising or some other bloody important thing. All those words I've bottled would fail me.

I'd lose courage, hang up, wouldn't I? There is no busload of casualties, no victims from a raging fire, no collapsed building. I just *need* to know. I'm not a victim of just another burnt dinner, a bruised heart, a collapsing marriage. This is a matter of life, an urgency. Yes Goddamit - it *is* an emergency.

We could move on, surely we could. Leave this lonely togetherness in the past. We're young enough, still. Just about. But we could, if we got things moving. Learn Chinese or Russian or Bulgarian or the language of whatever country the Agency advises. We could come unstuck somehow from this Limbo nothingness with the uncreated, this cyclical charting, where every high is a new low, a failure.

Do you really think you're God? I would ask. Do you also have your reasons? Four hundred million hopeless reasons floundering in a seminal sea? Why - won't - you - tell - me?

What if I dial now, right now and insist… if I ask on loudspeaker? Would he tell me then, all eyes on him? I wouldn't… surely… couldn't… But then, could there be a better place to corner him than in theatre, under lights, with an audience who can't walk out?

And he's good with words, no stranger to breaking bad news. Excels at it in fact. Well, spit it out for God's sake. For our sake.

Infusions

Sometimes these things just happen. Nobody's fault.
Funny, he must have used the correct word there
countless times while cutting, inadvertently practicing.
What's once more in God's greater scheme of things?

And sterile is such a sanitized word, essential for proper
aseptic technique.

An excellent way for a surgeon to be after all, isn't it?

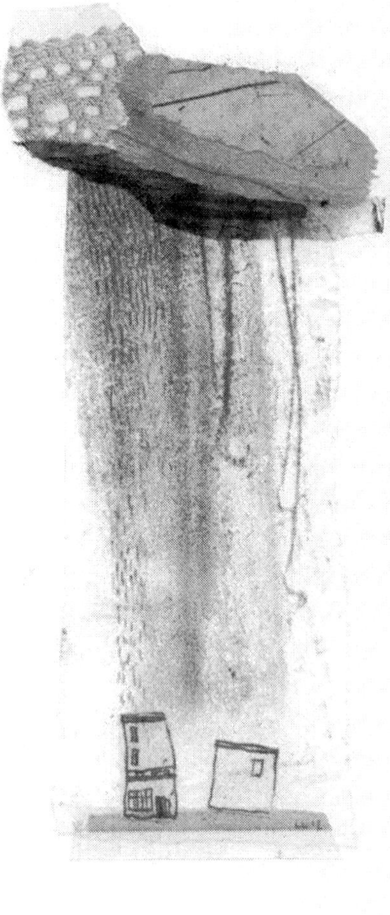

Infusions

Haiku
Fleur Finlay

Silent snowflakes fall
On the windscreen and dissolve
-Others take their place.

The wind
Whistles in the garden
-a birch tree dances.

White dust falls softly
On cars, windowsills and trees
unnatural snow

Through broken bottles
And gunfire cracking the sky
-a white handkerchief

Over the wall of
graffiti and barbed wire
the same sun rises

Java Writers

Infusions

JAVA WRITERS
AND ILLUSTRATORS

Java Writers

Biographies:

Fiona Scoble moved to Galway in January 2012 because she wasn't being rained on enough in Manchester. Her school careers advice programme selected "fish-sorter" as her optimum employment; she has spent years avoiding this fate, working as a journalist, artist, and arts project manager, but now being so close to the sea is reconsidering her vocation. She was longlisted in the 2012 Over The Edge New Writer of the Year Competition and was thrilled to be an Over The Edge featured reader in November 2012.

A. P. Kenny was born in County Galway in the 1940s. After a long career in I.T. she is now retired and lives in Galway city. She joined a creative writing class two years ago. She was longlisted in the 2012 Powers Short Story competition.

J.G. Lacey is a native of Tipperary and lived in Dublin for many years before moving to Galway with his wife, son and daughter. His children moved back to Dublin to get away from him. His wife, however, can't escape. This is his first published work.

Flish McCarthy is a poet, healer and grandmother living in Salthill. As a poet she has the craic pulling a few sweet sounds and images from the silence. As a practitioner of the healing arts of Healing Touch and Reiki, she creates a stable field for clients to achieve their own healing. As a mother and grandmother, she finds an abiding happiness. She loves her life.

Duana Sala is a graduate of Literature and Languages from the Università Cà Foscari, Venice, Italy. Born in Italy in 1981, she moved to Galway in 2008, following her deep wild passion for Ireland. She is currently writing her first novel.

Margaret Brady moved to Galway from Dublin in 1996. It was only meant to be for one year, but Galway stole her heart. She shares her home with her two college going children, an energetic dog and four and a half cats.

Bern Butler is a native Galwegian who has had an interest in writing, all of her life - achieving some success recently at competition level. She has worked in Prison Education for many years. She lives in the country, along with her family and three thought-provoking cats.

Phillipa Maguire Who or what am I but a speck of dust dissolving in time.

Bernadette Whyte began creative writing classes in early 2011. Since then she has been exploring different styles and genres. She joined Java writers over a year ago and feels her writing benefits from the support of the group. Her favourite thing about writing is how her characters often surprise her in the story.

Lorna Moynihan was born in Dublin and spent the first 12 years of her life there. In the 1970s the family moved to Galway, where Lorna grew up in a family of seven children. She has lived in Germany and Australia. She has worked in education for the past 14 years. She now lives in Galway with her husband and their three grown up children. She is an avid reader, and has always dreamed of being a writer. She joined a class in creative writing in Galway and this is her first published short story.

Infusions

Ann Flynn is a figment of many imaginations, all of whom are devotees of the Hindu god, Shiva.

Yvonne McEvaddy lives and works in Headford, County Galway. She is the author of two novels, *Passion Killer*, and *Shadows of the Dead*, both available on amazon. She is currently working on her third novel, *Thief of Hearts*. Yvonne has been longlisted in the Over The Edge New Writer of the Year competition.

Evelyn Parsons was commended in the Over The Edge New Writer of the Year Competition in 2010. In 2011, she won third place, also being awarded Ennis Bookclub Festival's Runner-up prize, and a place on the Fish One Page Prize long-list. She was honoured to be an OTE Featured Reader in Galway City Library, and read at the Crannog 29 Launch. In 2012 she was shortlisted for the Cúirt Literary Festival Showcase Reading. Her work was published in the Irish Times, Ballinasloe Life and Crannóg Magazine. She's a member of the Booksuckers Club in Ballinasloe, where she lives, and attempts to write fiction, fuelled by resounding encouragement from her husband Vincent and wonderful children - Jack, Fintan, Sally, and Béibhinn.

Lara Luxardi was born in Italy in 1989. She is a graduate of the Academy of Fine Arts of Venice. In the past few years she has been living and working between Venice, Pordenone, Valencia and Galway. Her illustrations and photographs have been exhibited in several individual and group exhibitions both in Italy and Ireland.

Fleur Finlay is originally from Portumna and now lives in Galway City. She has a degree in music and English literature from NUI Maynooth. Fleur plays the piano and is a Shakespeare enthusiast.

Java Writers

The Java Writers can be contacted at:
JAVASWRITERS@hotmail.com

Made in the USA
Charleston, SC
26 November 2012